ASSETS AND LIABILITIES

AN ALEX MASON THRILLER

DAVID ARCHER

BLAKE BANNER

RIGHTHOUSE

ISBN-13: 978-1-63696-085-2

ISBN-10: 1-63696-085-5

Cover design by: Damonza

Printed in the United States of America

www.righthouse.com

www.instagram.com/righthousebooks

www.facebook.com/righthousebooks

twitter.com/righthousebooks

PRAISE FOR ALEX MASON

"It is brutal, wastes no time, and is full of action."

"Better than Bond, Bourne, or Reacher."

AMAZON REVIEW

"For fans of Clancy, Mitch App, and Brad Taylor."

AMAZON REVIEW

"Same level as Patterson or Baldacci."

AMAZON REVIEW

"This book is filled with action, intrigue, espionage, and everything else lovers of a good thriller want."

AMAZON REVIEW

ALEX MASON THRILLERS

PROLOGUE

Mira Finn was uncharacteristically cold-blooded for an Irishwoman.

It was the kind of 20th-century, racist, misogynistic comment Nero, the director of ODIN, was fond of making while stuffing his face with gourmet food and drink. It didn't bother her. She tended to agree. Most of the Irish people she had grown up with in Dublin had been pretty hot-blooded, the women more than the men. She had never understood why they got so excited, far less the things they got excited about: clean socks, clean knickers, a clean front room. Cleanliness was generally involved. She didn't feel anything about cleanliness. She didn't feel anything about most things.

She selected one of several prepaid cell phones which she had bought the day before at Start Marais on Rue Vieille de Temple. She dialed a number she had been given. It rang three times and a man's voice spoke with a French accent.

"Hallo, who is calling, please?"

"Is that Amazon deliveries? I'm phoning about a package I am supposed to receive today. I wonder if I could change the delivery location."

"Yes, of course. Where would you like the package delivered?"

"Can you deliver it to Café Le Rostand, Place Edmond Rostand?"

"No problem, madame. Shall I deliver it at the bar?"

"No, I'll be sitting on the terrace with a copy of the *New York Herald Tribune* on the table. Four o'clock this afternoon."

A brief snort. "*Le Carré vit encore*. Sixteen hour."

The voice hung up.

Mira showered, changed her clothes and at three PM went for a stroll down Boulevard Saint-Michel as far as the Port Royal metro station. There she bought a Herald Tribune and made her way back up the boulevard to the café, where she sat outside in the early spring sunshine, ordered a glass of cold white wine and settled to read the paper. It was three forty-five.

At five minutes past four a dark Audi pulled up. The passenger door opened and a man with very short hair and a leather jacket climbed out. As the man moved in among the tables, the car pulled away to park farther up the road. Mira watched the man approach her table. He smiled. He spoke with an American accent.

"Good afternoon. Do you mind if I join you?"

"Actually I am expecting someone."

"I think I am the man you're expecting. The Amazon delivery guy?"

She felt nothing, but had a momentary flash of Nero

calling her cold-blooded. "I have no idea what you are talking about. But you are intruding on my privacy, so I would thank you to move along."

He gave a small laugh. "No need to get touchy. We actually need to talk."

He pulled out the chair and sat. She watched him do it and still felt nothing like fear or panic, though she knew perhaps she should.

"I wouldn't recommend telling the waiter to get rid of me, or calling the cops. You really do need to hear what I have to say."

"Who are you?"

He smiled. "You can call me Joe. I am a friend of Peter's."

"Peter?"

The smile faded from his face. "You are waiting for Peter, right?"

She sighed and glanced at the waiter, wondering what her next move should be.

"Look, uh, Joe. Either you're out of your mind or you have mistaken me for somebody else. Either way you're spoiling my afternoon. So I am going to ask you to move along."

He reached in his pocket and pulled out a cell phone which he placed on the table in front of her. An audio file began to play.

"'Hallo, who is calling, please?' 'Is that Amazon deliveries? I'm phoning about a package I am supposed to receive today. I wonder if I could change the delivery location.' 'Yes, of course. Where would you like the package delivered?' 'Can you deliver it to Café Le Rostand, Place Edmond

Rostand?' 'No problem, madame. Shall I deliver it at the bar?' 'No, I'll be sitting on the terrace with a copy of the New York Herald Tribune on the table. Four o'clock this afternoon.' 'Le Carré vit encore. Sixteen hour.'"

It stopped and Joe reached over and retrieved the phone. He didn't say anything. He seemed to search for something on his cell, then pressed the screen with his thumb, and a moment later her burner began to ring in her bag. He smiled at her. "Oops! I really think we need to talk, Ms Finn."

Three people in the world, aside from her, knew why she was in Paris. They had deliberately done it that way. The president of the United States knew she was there and why. Nero, the Director of ODIN, and the man he described as his most trusted agent, Alex Mason. Nobody else was supposed to know.

She looked across the road at the Luxembourg Gardens. There was a growing warmth in her gut. She didn't know whether it was fear or rage, but it was a powerful feeling. She spoke quietly.

"You lay one finger on me and I will kick and scream and claw until the waiters drag you off me, by which time we will have cops crawling all over this café like flies over a dead Russian. I suggest you take your phone and mince your tight little fanny out of here, Joe, before we end up causing an international incident."

He nodded. "OK." He thumbed the cell, called a number and muttered something, then hung up and slipped the phone into his inside pocket. When his hand reemerged it was holding a leather wallet. Out of the corner of her eye Mira saw the dark Audi backing down the street, emitting a high whine. As it drew level Joe stood, holding the open wallet high in the air with his left hand, shouting, "Gendarmerie Nationale! Gendarmerie Nationale!"

In his right hand he had a gun. He fired once into the air. Suddenly everybody was screaming and running. The doors of the Audi were flung open and three large, athletic men were descending on her.

She screamed, smashed her wineglass and stabbed hard at Joe's face with it. He bellowed with rage and she shouldered past him at a run, but ran straight into three men the size of small redwood trees. They scooped her up and carried her kicking and screaming across the sidewalk and bundled her into the back of the Audi, while the waiters and the customers at the café looked on and wondered what to do. Joe climbed into the front passenger seat pressing a white napkin to his torn face. The napkin was rapidly turning red. "Gendarmerie Nationale!" he shouted one more time, and the car accelerated away with a squeal of tires.

Nobody took the number of the license plate.

Sprawled across the two men on the back seat, Mira felt a sharp stab in her ass, and for a moment felt intense emotion. Her belly burned and she was aware of an intense need to leave the car. She heard the engine accelerate, tried to move and found she could not.

———

THE NEXT THING she was aware of was a feeling of nausea. As her eyes opened she found she was in the dark. Her hands hurt badly and so did her feet. She tried to move them but could not. She was sitting, and as awareness returned in the blackness, she realized she was tied to a chair. For a moment her cold blood became ice, and a moment later it was molten terror.

She had no idea how long she waited. Time has no meaning in absolute blackness. But by the time she heard the key turning in the padlock she had been through screaming rage, sobbing grief, pleading fear and numbness.

When the doors opened she found she was in a steel container of the sort used to transport goods on trucks and ships. A spotlight glared in her eyes, blinding her, and she turned away, squeezing her eyes tight. When she opened them again it was to find she was in a dentist's chair. Her hands and her feet were purple and swollen from having been tied too tight too long, with mountaineering bootlaces.

A silhouette appeared in the doorway, slightly amorphous against the bright light outside. He seemed to be carrying something in his hands. It was a small, metal table and it rattled as he set it down. He pulled on some surgical gloves and stepped closer to her, leaning forward with his hands on his knees. She realized there must be a bulb above her head, because a halo of dull light illuminated his features. His eyes were squinting. His mouth, framed by a scraggy moustache and beard, was slightly open and creased into a smile.

"Are we wakey-wake?"

"Please don't do this. This is not necessary."

He laughed. It was an ugly chortle. He held up a large, crumpled ball of blue and white linen.

"You know what is this?"

She gave her head a minute shake. She was aware her heart was racing and she felt sick.

"Is butcher's apron."

He turned and walked away, morphing into a hazy form in the glow of the spotlight as he slipped the apron over his head. Her mind was racing too fast for her to hold on to the thoughts. Her mind was full of a screaming voice telling her it could not find a solution.

Another form appeared in the door and walked toward her with slow steps. When he spoke his accent was American.

"It looks like you're in a lot of trouble, Mira."

"Just tell me what you want. I am not a hero."

"That's good to know."

"I swear, I will do anything."

"OK."

He moved to the side and returned with a chair. He sat and his face came into the halo of light. She went very cold inside. It was a cold that was beyond ice. It vanquished all hope. He smiled.

"This changes things a bit, doesn't it, Mira?"

All she could think to say was, "What do you want?"

"I want to know who ODIN's contacts are in Moscow."

"I know some of them. Only Nero knows all of them. But I can find out."

"Good. Recite the ones you know. This is being recorded. But, Mira—" He paused. "Do remember that if you lie, we will find out."

"I won't lie."

And as she said it, grief, shame and humiliation made her weep. She spoke, and once she had started she could not stop. She gave him everything she knew, including the whereabouts of Peter Rusenko, the Amazon packet she was supposed to collect, and the contacts who were supposed to bring him to her.

When she was done the man went to stand. She said, "Wait! There is more."

"More?"

"I can be of use to you. Nobody has ever penetrated ODIN. Send me back. I am trusted. I can supply you with information from the highest levels. I can keep you posted on practically every ODIN operation that is executed."

He frowned with his eyebrows and smiled with his lips, then sat back and crossed one leg over the other.

"Seriously? What do you think your worth will be to ODIN once Rusenko is captured, tried and executed?"

"Don't! Let me take him in. My stock will rise in ODIN, I can get closer to Nero, and at the same time I can run Rusenko. I will tailor what information he gives the Americans, and channel information from him back to you about what projects they have him working on."

He chuckled. "How stupid do you think I am, Mira? You really think I am going to let you go through with your original plan?"

A small ember of hope began to glow in her belly.

"Yes, I admit, it's a ploy for you to set me free and get out of this with all my limbs and my life intact. But think about it. You are still in time. Right now, in this moment, you own one of ODIN's top operatives. How often are you going to get that opportunity? You can destroy me any time you like. I have no choice but to do everything you tell me. And not only that, you are going to have one of Russia's leading scientists positioned within an American defense program, handled by me. OK, it's a ploy for me to get out of here alive. But it also happens to be a golden opportunity for you."

The smirk slowly evaporated from his face and his eyes became distracted. He pulled a pack of Camels from his pocket, pinched one free and lit up. He sat there, thinking, inhaling the smoke deep into his lungs until the cigarette was practically down to the filter. Then he looked at Mira, thrust out his bottom lip and nodded. The ember of hope in her belly sprouted flames, but she fought not to show it. The man stood and walked out into the glow from the spotlight. For a moment nothing happened. Then another shadow morphed through the glare. It was the leering form of the man in the butcher's apron.

From where he stood at the door to the warehouse, the American heard the scream. It was a horrible, inhuman sound. Worse. It was the sound of a living being losing its humanity. Somewhere, deep inside, a residual part of him was glad the United States no longer did this kind of thing. But he also recognized this was the very reason Russia was growing in strength and would soon be swarming all over Europe, while the pussies in NATO peed in their frilly panties and developed non-lethal weapons. The game goes to the meanest son of a bitch in the valley. That was a lesson he had learned a long time ago.

————

DAWN CAME GRAY AND COLD. On the Ile de la Cité, between the Pont Notre-Dame and the Pont d'Arcole, gray, granite steps descended to the frigid water opposite the Hôtel-Dieu. Trash and green slime tended to accumulate around the base of those steps. So it was past seven thirty before anybody noticed that among the slime and the trash there was something else. A green blouse was pointed out by one person to another. Then dark jeans were spotted, and finally red hair that moved softly on the ripples of the water. The river police were the first to dispatch a unit, and it was they who found that it was a young woman who had been cruelly mutilated.

Half an hour later the BRI—the Brigade de Recherche et d'Intervention—had cordoned off that section of the Quai de la Corse, and the steps down to the river. Blue lights flashed and pulsed in the dull morning against the gray stone walls and on the gray murk of the Seine.

The medical examiner had made his preliminary examination on the lower steps, by the water. Then the body had been carried with difficulty up to the sidewalk, where they had zipped it into a body bag before wheeling it into the ambulance. Then the blue, pulsing lights had started mournfully to disperse. Some of them returned to police headquarters, and others to the morgue.

ONE

LOVELOCK HAD CALLED ME AT NOON FROM A burner, which was unusual. Lovelock called always from the office on the secure line. She had given me verbal instructions in less than thirty seconds and hung up without allowing me to reply. The instructions were not so much complicated as convoluted. So much so that I had written them down as soon as she had hung up, in order to give myself time to memorize them properly.

It had involved going for a walk to McMillan Park and then continuing on to Columbia Heights where I would get the Metro to Chinatown, switch trains and go to L'Enfant Plaza where I had to switch again to the Metro Center, return to Gallery Place in Chinatown and travel north to U Street.

After that, if I was satisfied I had not been followed, I was to take a circuitous route, on foot, via V Street and T Street, to Vernon Street, to a safe house we had there.

It was unusual. But then, I told myself, Nero was

nothing if not a man of contradictions. On the one hand he was obsessive about routine and detested change, yet he was one of the most unpredictable men I had ever met. The key was of course that his attacks of unpredictability tended to affect *other* people's routines, not his.

This time, once again, was different.

The house on Vernon Street was a small, Georgian redbrick with a sage green door at the top of thirteen steps. I was vaguely aware as I climbed them that thirteen steps in DC generally suggested some historical connection with the Man Himself and those who had laid the foundation stones of the New Atlantis.

I knocked on the door and it was opened by a man I had never seen before. To say he appeared aloof would be like saying the Antarctic was chilly. He had a nose a hawk would envy, eyebrows that could look down on their own forehead, a white chef's coat and a regal bearing to shame kings. He gazed at me like I was an insult and he was awaiting my apology. Following Lovelock's instructions I said, "Did you advertise a dining table for sale?"

He groaned softly as he sighed and replied, "We 'ave only a Queen Anne, perraps it is too refined for monsieur."

"Queen Anne will do fine."

"*Eh bien*, please, come in." He stepped back and closed the door behind me. "Follow me, *s'il vous plaît.*"

I followed him across a tiled floor to a door on the left. He knocked with the back of his knuckle, stared at the ceiling until Nero's voice called, "Enter!" and opened the door for me.

I was not surprised to find myself in a dining room. There was a long, mahogany table. Nero considered tablecloths vulgar and middle class, so he had two placemats. He was at the head of the table with a view of the heavy, burgundy drapes that had been drawn across the window. A fire burned in a Georgian, marble fireplace and there was a bottle of white wine open in a bucket of ice on the table.

Nero did not stand. He nudged his knife with his fingernail and said, "You're late."

"I was escaping from ghosts. Besides, you didn't give a time."

"Sit down. I assume you haven't eaten."

"Manny Pacquiao is eating my beef ragout as we speak."

He stared at me blankly. "The boxer?"

"My cat."

"We have a turbot mousse and salmon mousse with a nice Gewürztraminer." As he said it he tucked a large linen napkin into his collar. "After that we have lamb broiled in honey and eucalyptus, with a nice 2016 Chateau Clinet. As I am sure you know, 2016 was a superb year in Bordeaux."

"You had mentioned it."

"Are you going to sit down, or do you intend to eat standing up, like one of those people one sees outside Metro stations?"

I sat and draped my napkin on my left knee. He extracted the bottle from the ice and poured me a glass.

"Sir, I believe this is one of the very few times I have ever seen you outside your office. And though we have eaten in the same room before, this is the first time you have invited me to lunch."

"Your point being that these two exceptional circumstances imply an exceptional cause."

"Yes, and also, why the very convoluted meeting? Couldn't I have simply gone to the office, as I always do?"

"No. Clearly not."

The door opened and the man with the enviable nose delivered two plates, each containing two mousse, one pink and one white. He delivered also a basket of crackers, and refilled our glasses. Nero waved his fingers at him in a "go away" sort of gesture.

"Thank you, Lucas. I'll call you when we are ready."

Lucas bowed and left.

"How do you manage to stay in the nineteenth century without getting caught and sent back?"

He looked at me with a trace of a smile but didn't answer.

"Alex, ODIN is seriously compromised." I spread salmon mousse on a cracker and waited for him to go on. "Mira was caught. Her body was pulled from the Seine yesterday morning. She had been badly tortured. We must assume she told them everything she knew."

"How much did she know?"

"Too much, but that, as it turns out, is the least of our worries." He waved his hand at my starter and said, "Enjoy in silence while I fill you in. You can ask questions later."

We chewed a moment. He sipped and went on.

"Now, facts, Dr. Rusenko is on the run. I received a very brief telephone call from him the day before yesterday at three PM Paris time. He said that he had not received the call he was expecting from Mira Finn. Yet, a little earlier we had received confirmation from her that contact had been made and she was going to arrange a meeting. Correct codes had been used. When we attempted to contact Mira she could not be found, and her telephone seemed to be turned off."

"Did you send someone to look for her?"

"As you know agents have operational discretion as far as is possible. It was down to her to arrange the handover point, and it was essential that as few people as possible knew where that would be. In this case, in theory, it was Mira, Rusenko and his Paris contact. Had she checked in as she was supposed to, then I would have known too. But she didn't. We later found out from the BRI—"

"The BRI?"

"The *Brigade de Recherche et d'Intervention*," he said in an annoyingly perfect French accent, "that a woman fitting Mira's description had been abducted from the Café Le Rostand, on the Place Edmond Rostand. The café is a twenty-minute walk from her apartment and would have been a suitable place for the handover. It remains unclear what prevented her from communicating to me where the handover would take place."

"Description of the abductors?"

"Dark Audi, four large, fit men in jeans and leather jackets, claiming to be policemen. They pulled her from her table and forced her into the back of the vehicle, then took off south. That of course gives us no indication whatever of where they took her."

"Sir, this raises some pretty tough questions."

"Indeed."

"Correct me if I am wrong, but to the best of my knowledge, very few people knew Mira was in Paris, and only four knew why. If the Russians knew that Mira was there to collect Dr. Rusenko, it means that one of those four people told them."

"You are absolutely correct, Alex. The fact that Rusenko did not receive the communication from her, the fact that I did not receive her call, and the fact that she was snatched from an obvious handover point all suggest that her phone had been compromised, and that they knew she was there to receive Rusenko." He wagged his knife. "But here is a thing: They did *not* know where Rusenko was, or how to get to him. Remember, Rusenko is a highly intelligent man. He enjoys Le Carré and Len Deighton in the original English and does the *Daily Telegraph* cryptic crossword every morning in ten to fifteen minutes."

I stared at him blankly for a moment. "So, they took her to find out where he was, but he had already been alerted by not hearing from her, and he vanished." I scratched my head. "But why not allow her to make the call to Rusenko, set up the meet and snatch them both?"

"Because, I imagine, they feared that once Mira and Rusenko made contact, that would be communicated to us along with the handover location and we and the CIA would be all over them. They hoped that by snatching her they might be able to find out his whereabouts and snatch him before we could respond."

I nodded and drained my glass. As I set it down I said, "OK, that makes sense. So we are left looking for the leak. And the leak has to be either you, General Patrick O'Connor, the president of the United States or me."

"That is about the size of it, Alex, yes."

The door opened and Lucas brought in a dish of lamb, which he uncovered and proceeded to carve and serve on a bed of potatoes fried in olive oil and garlic and garnished with absolutely nothing because it didn't need it, and nobody present was likely to be offended by the absence of lettuce.

Lucas poured the wine and withdrew. We ate in reverent silence for a while. Eventually Nero pointed at the lamb and spoke with his mouth full.

"Lucas. He cooks this. He is very good."

I nodded and, a while later, I drained my glass and slid it across the table to him.

"So, as I understand it, I have two objectives."

He refilled our glasses and muttered, "Tell me."

"Find Rusenko before the Russians do, and find the leak."

"Well, the leak is fairly obvious. Your objective is a little more complex than you see it."

"The leak is obvious?"

"I can see I need to draw you a picture, Alex. Objectively —and the only people in this situation capable of being truly objective are you and I—objectively the leak is easy to identify. However, from the president's perspective, and from General O'Connor's perspective, it is equally obvious who the leak is."

I sat back and picked up my glass. "You're going to have to spell it out, sir."

"The leak is either General O'Connor, or the president. The president is very unlikely because at his level of power things are done differently. However, General O'Connor might well be in the pay of Moscow. He is an able man and he is an advisor to the president, but he has been passed over a couple of times for high-prestige posts and he harbors resentment against colleagues and former administrations. If Putin offered him enough, he might well take the bait.

"However, that being the case, he would need a scapegoat." He stared at me for a long moment and I felt my skin going cold. He nodded. "Yes, Alex, you are the scapegoat. I had intended to make you a part of this mission because you are my best man, but he specifically requested you be part of the team anyway. He had you lined up to take the fall from the start."

"So, sir, am I under arrest? Is that why I am here?"

"Don't be absurd. You are here because we need to hammer out the details of your mission. Your first priority is to find Dr. Rusenko and deliver him to ODIN. Your second objective is to establish precisely where the leak is, and uncover the chain of communication from the Kremlin to the White House. That chain will lead to O'Connor's accomplices and contacts in Washington. Aside from anything else, Alex, it is the only way to clear your name."

We finished the lamb and the wine in silence. When we were finished I wiped my mouth and dropped the napkin on the table.

"It will be very difficult for you to provide me with help."

"Very difficult indeed, Alex. However, before you go I shall provide you with a cell phone with which you can communicate with me. But you must keep that communication to an absolute minimum."

"Thank you, sir."

"I also have a file for you to study and some documents you can use, passport, et cetera. You will have to go to Paris, of course." He sighed. "Aside from that I am afraid you are pretty much on your own, and in any case it is probably preferable that I do not know what you are doing, or how you are going about it."

I nodded. "Understood."

"Now, some cheese, a little whiskey, and you had better be on your way."

AN HOUR later I left the safe house as the afternoon was turning to copper, and walked the four hundred yards to the Washington Hilton on Connecticut Avenue. There I checked in using the documents Nero had provided me with, and went up to my room to study the scant information he'd been able to give me. It was about forty percent fact and sixty percent opinion. On the plus side, when you got to know Nero, you realized that most of the time his opinion was worth more than the facts. I dined at the hotel, had an early night and, in the morning I took a cab to my bank on G Street, opposite the Metro Center Station.

When I climbed from the taxi, the air was fresh and early-morning cool in the shade of the trees. They might have been pin oaks, or maples, or London plane trees. I promised myself yet again, as I paced the sidewalk in the morning air, that when I had more time I would learn all the names of common trees and plants. So if I ever had grandchildren I could take them for informative country walks, and look wise.

A young woman appeared within the bank, hunkered down on the other side of the big, glass doors and unlocked them. I stopped pacing, grunted a quiet smile and told myself that my ever having grandchildren was about as likely as Nero becoming vegan and adopting "Namaste" as a greeting.

Once inside I had a quiet word with the cashier, who had a quiet word with an assistant manager who in turn had a quiet word with a security guard. Then the security guard and the assistant manager had a quiet word with me and took me quietly down some carpeted stairs to an elevator which descended a couple of floors to a red-carpeted basement that smelt of wax furniture polish. There, I was taken down a short passage to a small room with a steel door. The assistant manager and the security guard each had a key. They unlocked the door and stood aside while I went into the small vault to withdraw my safety deposit box.

Not all safety deposit boxes are that well guarded, but you get what you pay for, and I paid over the odds for this one. This had nothing to do with ODIN. They knew nothing about it. This was mine, one of several I had around the world, and I thought of it as an emergency survival kit.

It contained an attaché case with a hundred thousand dollars in untraceable bills, a passport in the name of Samuel Silver, a driver's license and a Mastercard Black. It also contained a sealed plastic bag with a fake moustache, hair dye, glasses and shaving equipment, just in case. There were other bits and pieces, like a couple of prepaid burners and some electronic toys, but mainly it was the basic essentials. I figured that if I was going to be on the run for a while, it was best not even ODIN knew who I was or where I was.

I checked the contents, snapped the case shut and left the bank to take a walk up 11th Street to the Starbucks at the Grand Hyatt. There I had a double espresso and a croissant, and used one of the burners to contact Aila Gallin in London.

"What?"

"Hello darling, I thought you'd be pleased to hear from me."

"Oh, it's you. It just said United States on the screen. I thought Microsoft was trying to sell me something again."

"Well, you know how it is, kiddo, we all have problems..."

I let the words linger and she caught them.

"Yeah? Anything I can do?"

"Oh, you know, it's the usual stuff. You're lucky, you have a very supportive family. I mean, I doubt they'd be interested in my problems. But my family? Man! They just leave me out in the cold."

"Holy shit! Are you serious?"

I laughed. "You know how it is. Your cousin upsets everybody and you end up getting the blame. But listen, I don't want to burden you with my woes."

"Don't be stupid. Can you make it to London?"

"Oh, that would be swell. Might be a couple of days. But just keep it between you and me, OK? I wouldn't want to offend Aunt Aggie."

"You got it. Call me and I'll collect you at the airport."

"You're a doll."

I hung up, left the warm smell of morning coffee and cakes and went out into the morning to hail a cab.

TWO

I HAD THE TAXI TAKE ME TO THE STELLAR SMILES
dentist's surgery on Pennsylvania Avenue, South East, on the
far side of the Anacostia River divide. I paid off the cab and
watched him drive away. Then, when he was out of sight, I
walked the three hundred yards to the intersection with
Minnesota Avenue, and crossed over to the post office. I
didn't go in, I walked around it, down a narrow alley with
no name, among dilapidated backyards fenced off with bits
of moldy ply, old bed frames and car doors. At the end of a
stretch of chicken wire I came to another, shorter alley on
the right. This one was flanked either side by eighteen broad,
squat lockups painted a nasty turmeric yellow and finished
off with lots of chrome graffiti.

I walked down among the roller blinds, found number
nine and unlocked it. When I rolled up the door, there was a
sharp smell of old, musty dust. A large blue tarp covered a
bulky, amorphous object that took up most of the floor. I
pulled back the plastic and revealed the 2010 Toyota Camry.

It was clean and in perfect condition. It only needed a battery. The battery was in the corner, connected to a charger which clicked on automatically every four weeks. The car was not intended to be used. It had been sitting there for three years. Once a year I took it to a mechanic in Deanwood for a checkup, but aside from that it just sat here in the lockup, waiting for a day such as this.

I rolled up my sleeves, fitted the battery and fired up the engine. It started the first time. I rolled out into the alley, wiped my prints off the door, locked it and pulled out onto Pennsylvania Avenue.

I took a circuitous route via Hyattsville and the University of Maryland golf course to pick up the I-95 at Cherry Hill Park. After that it was pretty much a four-hour straight run all the way to New York.

I followed the I-95 across the George Washington Bridge and the Alexander Hamilton Bridge, and then took the Cross Bronx Expressway as far as the Bronx River Parkway interchange. I followed Soundview Avenue as far as Harding Park, practically on the water, where you'd be forgiven for thinking you were not in New York at all, but in some remote part of New England. The houses are a jumble of shapes and sizes with clapboard walls and gabled roofs, tucked in among abundant trees and huge lawns.

There, I tucked into Husson Avenue and parked outside a small, peculiar house at the end of the road. It had a big garage and cast-iron steps leading up to the two-storey living quarters above. It stood alone in its own, overgrown plot, and had plenty of trees to seclude it.

It was a bit extravagant, but I'd figured ten years earlier, when I'd bought the place, that maybe someday I'd need somewhere only I knew about. It was a part of my survival pack. In my game, far-sightedness can be a life-saving virtue —and anyhow, property in New York is always an invest-ment, right?

I stuck the Toyota in the garage and took the internal staircase to the living room and kitchen, on the first floor above the garage. The cupboards were bare and the place smelt damp and musty. The only stores were a six-pack of beers and a bottle of scotch. I hadn't been there for over six months, and that had been no more than a stop-over.

I checked my watch. It was four PM, nine PM in London. I grabbed a cold beer from the fridge and climbed the stairs to the bedroom. There I had a desktop with a sophisticated scrambler and VPN which made it almost impossible to trace. I sat down, switched on the computer and called Gallin.

After a moment her face appeared on the screen. The room she was in was dark and her face was ghostly, illumi-nated only by the screen she was looking at. She was frowning.

"What the hell's going on?"

"I need your help. But it is a very delicate matter."

"I can do delicate. What is it?"

"We lost an agent in Paris. She was abducted and tortured."

"Shit. Arabs?"

"No. Russians."

"Those guys are insane. You know they're planning to take Poland and the Baltic states, right?"

"Yeah, I know. Listen. We had her in Paris to collect a package, but here's the rub. Only four people knew why she was there. Nero, General Patrick O'Connor, the president and me."

Her mouth formed a big, silent O.

"Yeah, I'm the scapegoat."

"Nero?"

"He's doing what he can to help."

"What do you want me to do?"

I took a pull on the beer. It was cold and slightly bitter. "OK, I need to find the package—"

"It wasn't snatched?"

"No. The agent was snatched and the package went AWOL. The package is smart, so he won't be easy to find."

"Unless he wants to be."

"Yeah, maybe. But most of all I need to find the person in Paris who was liaising with..."

I hesitated a moment and she said, "General O'Connor, or the president."

I sighed. "Yeah, it sounds absurd. But the bottom line is, one of them has to be working with the Russians, and alerted them to the fact that our agent was in Paris; and why she was there. That means they had a contact in Paris. I need to find that contact and make him or her talk."

She nodded and thrust out her bottom lip.

"OK, I see that. But where the hell do we begin?"

"All I can think of at the moment is Mira's apartment."

"Mira? That's the agent?"

"Mira Finn. I shouldn't be telling you this."

"You're the scapegoat, Mason. The rules change. First you were an asset. Now you're a liability."

I grunted. She had a point. "OK, her apartment and then the medical report."

She frowned and screwed up her nose for good measure. "The medical report? What for?"

"Trust me. I have a hunch. Can you pull strings through your contacts in Paris and get me a copy of the report?"

"Yeah, I can probably do that. It's risky. If you have enemies at the level of generals, presidential advisers and presidents wanting to bring you down as the scapegoat, chances are they'll have figured already you'll go for her apartment and the ME's report."

"I know," I sighed, "that's my hunch. The point is, do they know that I know that they know?"

She frowned. "I don't know."

"So, if you can ask your contact to deliver the copy of the report to Mr. Samuel Silver at Rue de Latran number eight, in Paris, that would be a big help."

"What is that, like, Toilet Street?"

"No, Gallin, Latran comes from Lateran, which was the name given to a number of buildings in Rome because they were owned by the Lateranus family during the time of the Roman Empire. The Emperor Constantine took their properties away from them and gave them to the Catholic Church, in the year 311 AD."

"Oh. OK. I prefer my idea."

"So do I. I am going to try and get a flight to Paris tonight. So I should be there in anything between eight and twelve hours."

"You don't want to pass by London on the way, so we can talk?"

I thought about it. "That would be nice, Gallin. But I don't think it would be useful. I'd best get to Paris as soon as possible. I'll let you know my flight details as soon as I have them so you can inform your contact."

"Ten four. Keep me in the loop, Mason."

I hung up and set about booking a flight to Paris. I found an Air France departing at eight-thirty PM that night from JFK, arriving seven and a half hours later at Charles de Gaulle, at nine-fifty in the morning, local time.

I sent Gallin the flight details, had some lunch, packed a bag and, at five PM, I drove to the airport. All through Flushing and Queens I kept my eye on my rearview mirror. I was not aware of anybody following me. A couple of times I took circuitous routes just in case, but I wasn't followed and I arrived at the airport in time to check in and board pretty confident I had done so unnoticed.

I had a meal on board and a dry martini, then slept the rest of the way.

The stewardess woke me for breakfast and at nine thirty, slightly ahead of schedule, we touched down in Paris.

They had a Volvo XC40 ready for me at the car hire and, once the cute French attendant had got through making me sign papers, she gave me my key and allowed me to drive away into the French, spring morning. I took the A3 through the early sunshine and the kamikaze French drivers, thinking about the tragedy of the European Empire. There had been a time when France looked, sounded, and above all smelt, French. Cafés were places where you were deafened by the comforting screams of big, red Gaggia coffee machines and your nostrils were invaded by the homely smell of Gauloise, Gitanes and espresso coffee, while you trod across tiled floors littered with cigarette butts, mostly without filters. You knew you were in France.

No longer. Now you know you are in Europe. The Paris where beauty and rationalism lay tangled in sheets with humanism and logic on a bare mattress on a garret floor in Montmartre, lies in her twentieth-century grave, along with Matisse, Camus and Sartre. What Hitler and his gang of thugs were not able to do with bombs and tanks, the Euro-Empire achieved with Directives and Regulations. Absinthe and decadence was fine for them, back then, but the New European marches to a more standardized tune.

La France is dead, long live the Union.

With these sad thoughts in my mind, I did not go to my hotel. Instead I merged with the A1 and entered Paris from the north. Then, following the Rue de la Chaelle, I moved south through broad leafy streets, populated with kiosks and cafés that were still draped with the shades of old Paris, like ghosts reluctant to leave just yet.

It was pretty much a straight run past the Gare du Nord and the Gare de l'Est, south. I crossed the river at the very spot where Mira's body had been found, and then turned east to Rue de Latran. I smiled: Gallin's Toilet Street. I had to go around a couple of times, but eventually found a space outside the church at the end of the road and was able to park.

Number eight was halfway up on the right. It had large slatted French shutters and large wooden doors that led onto a cool, shaded checkerboard entrance hall with an attractive staircase and one of those concertina elevators with mirrors and brass lamps. I pressed the button for the fourth floor and wished I'd brought my fedora and my pencil moustache.

I stepped out onto a tiled landing with wrought-iron banisters. The door to her apartment was tall, broad and blue, with a big brass knob in the middle. Thirty seconds with a lockpick had the door open and I stepped inside.

There was a bright entrance hall with a free-standing, floor-to-ceiling mirror against the wall. A small stand held a vase of flowers and beside it there was a bentwood coat stand. A door on the left led into the kitchen with a pine table and a block of Sabatier knives. On the right a white door with stained-glass panes gave on to a large living room with a high ceiling and tasteful modern furniture of the sort IKEA doesn't quite make. The slatted shutters were open and I looked out at the street below, where the Parisians were being joyfully noisy with mopeds and car horns.

A second door led onto a long corridor with a bathroom on the right and two bedrooms on the left, each overlooking the street outside. The first had the shutters closed, the bed was unmade and the closet was empty. The second had an en suite bathroom with toiletries, a toothbrush and all the other things you'd expect to find in a woman's bathroom.

I sat on the bath and looked around. I had no idea what I was looking for and was hoping that the ninety percent of my mind that Freud said was unconscious, might give me a hand.

Mira's father was Irish, but her mother was French. She lived most of the time in London, but came frequently to the apartment her parents had left her in Paris. That was a good part of the reason Nero had chosen her for the handover—that and the fact she was a damned good pro.

Her job had been to make contact with the agent who would bring Rusenko to Paris from Poland, and from here take him to DC. The fact that she had failed to make contact with both Rusenko and Nero made it clear that she had been compromised. But the fact that instead of activating an escape protocol, she had gone to a café for a glass of wine suggested she did not know she had been compromised.

A moment's thought told you she thought she had made contact, and as far as she was concerned she *had* contacted Nero and Rusenko, and she believed the handover was going to take place at the café.

If that was the case it meant two things: one, her calls had been intercepted, and two, she had received fake replies which were good enough to convince her. In the case of Rusenko's contact in Paris, that was bad news, but it was not impossible to believe. In the case of Nero it was very serious, because it meant that either the Russians had somebody who could impersonate Nero well enough to convince Mira, which was hard to believe, or that they had obtained sufficient recordings of him to synthesize his voice. Which was easier to believe, but much more worrying.

I had to assume that in her calls Mira was using either a secure phone provided by ODIN, or disposable burners. Both would be extremely difficult to intercept.

Unless.

Unless there was a bug in the apartment that could communicate with any active cell phone in a given radius, acquire its data and divert any calls it made to given numbers. So if Mira called Nero, or Rusenko's mediator, the call would be diverted to a number set up by the Russian cell. There each call would be dealt with to set Mira up so they could snatch her and Rusenko. Obviously, it only half-worked.

It was a big unless, and for now all of it was speculation

on my part. But I knew enough about basic Bluetooth technology to know that it was at least a theoretical possibility.

I sighed and raised my ass off the bath. Right then I had only one way of knowing whether my theory was at least on the right track, and that was by finding the alleged bug.

The obvious places to look were in the landline and in the light fitments. A careful scrutiny of all those yielded nothing. After that it was a painstaking search of the entire apartment, giving precedence to places and areas that were unlikely to get swept, hovered or inspected with any kind of frequency. The undersides of tables and chairs, chests of drawers and stucco moldings, all yielded zilch, as did the backs of pictures and mirrors.

I was about to give up on my theory, while also toying with the idea of patenting the device I had obviously invented, when something caught my eye in the entrance hall. It was a wooden cupboard-like box of mock-Tyrolean design, attached to the wall just behind the free-standing, bentwood coat rack. I moved the coat rack and opened the door, which had a small, brass handle.

Inside was the fuse box, contained within a plastic housing with a plastic door. I opened that door too and found all the usual fuses plus the trip switch. After a moment's thought, I went around the apartment switching on all the lights and appliances. Then I went back to the fuse box and started methodically turning off and pulling out the fuses, one by one, and then putting them back in again, moving from left to right.

As you'd expect, one after another, the lights went out and the appliances switched off, only to come on again when I reconnected the fuses. Eventually, after a short time, I had disconnected and reconnected every electrical circuit in the apartment. And I still had one fuse left. That made me smile.

I pulled the last remaining fuse, telling myself it might just be a spare, perhaps intended for a larger apartment, or house. But it wasn't. There was a curious electronic device connected to it. It was not unlike a fuse, and unless you were actively looking for a bug, you would assume it was a fuse. But I knew better. Because I was actively looking for a bug. I smiled at it and said, "Hello."

That was when I heard the key in the lock. I dropped the bug in my pocket, closed the Tyrolean box and replaced the coat stand, all in one swift, fluid movement.

Then the door opened.

THREE

He had son of a bitch written all over his face. He was maybe thirty. He was tall, lean and strong. He had a slight curl to his lip, insolent pale blue eyes and antifreeze in his veins to keep the blood flowing. If reptiles could take human form, they would look like this guy.

He took a small step and his right fist smashed into my face. It caught me by surprise and sent me reeling across the hall and into the big mirror. While I was doing that he stepped inside, closed the door behind him and pulled a suppressed semi-automatic from under his jacket.

My head was swimming and the room was rocking. My hand seemed to act of its own accord, grabbed the flower vase and hurled it savagely at the SOB's face. He batted it aside with the pistol, which bought me all of half a second. It wasn't enough. I needed at least three quarters of a second to pull my weapon. I lunged at him instead, kicked him hard in the knee, pinned his gun hand to his chest and delivered a hard, hammering right hook to his jaw. He weaved away and it caught him in the ear instead. I held on to his wrist, twisted hard and smashed it on my knee. The pistol dropped.

He came back with a right cross to my face which hurt, and a left hook to my ribs which hurt more and sent me staggering back again. That was when he hesitated, just a fraction of a second. He wanted to pick up his gun, but thought I needed a couple more thumps to keep me down.

He was right.

I propelled myself off the wall like I was going to tear his face off. But instead I stamped at his knee again. It made him wince and withdraw his leg. So I kicked it again and as my foot touched the floor I ducked and hammered two powerful hooks, right and left, into his floating ribs. It would have floored Godzilla. It didn't floor this guy. It made him mad. He laid into my head with a series of combinations, driving me back toward the mirror. I covered my head with my forearms and took the barrage as I retreated.

When I felt the mirror behind me, I moved to my right slightly, inching into the kitchen, then lashed out with my foot at his knee again. That gave me a two-second breather where I reached out, grabbed the mirror and pulled it crashing down on his head.

The glass shattered and showered around him, making him scream with rage. Instinctively I reached for my piece to shoot at his legs. But I'd had to leave it in New York. I was not with ODIN anymore.

He hurled the mirror off. It hit the doorframe and crashed to the floor as he leapt over it and hit me hard in the head with his elbow. I parried a second blow from his left elbow with my left hand, fell back against the kitchen table and hammered at his head with my fist. It hurt him and blood flowed freely down his nose, but he grabbed a heavy, glass bottle of olive oil from the kitchen table and swung it savagely at my head. I leaned back and it grazed my shoulder. I pinned his arm against his chest again and headbutted him hard between the eyes, delivered a savage elbow to his face and reached behind me for the wooden block of Sabatier knives I'd seen earlier. He saw my intent and, shrieking with rage between clenched teeth, he smashed the bottle and stabbed viciously at my face. I felt the wooden handle in my hand, ducked and drove the big meat cleaver into his belly.

For a second he frowned at me, like he really wanted to tell me something about his life, how maybe it didn't make much sense right then, he had not expected this to be his future. But his pale blue eyes glazed and he slid to the floor. It was a shame. It would have been useful to talk to him.

I rummaged through his pockets and wasn't surprised to find absolutely nothing. So I searched the kitchen cabinets and found a plastic cup. I pressed his fingers onto it and slipped it into a plastic sandwich bag. Then I went to the bathroom, took a Q-tip and swabbed the blood that was seeping from his belly. I put that in a sandwich bag too. Then I cleaned myself up as best I could in front of the mirror, wiped my prints off everything I had touched and slipped out of the apartment.

I crossed back to the north side of the river, made my way to the Rue du Colonel Driant and dropped the car in an underground parking garage two blocks from the Louvre. From there I strolled the four hundred yards to the Louvre Gardens through the ancient streets with their tall, eighteenth-century buildings with elegant, shuttered windows. I took it slow and easy with my hands in my pockets, turning over what had happened in the apartment.

When I got to the gardens I moved away from the crowds, took a burner from my pocket and called Gallin.

"Did you get the report?"

"Things didn't work out the way I expected."

"You OK?"

"A little bruised, but aside from that, fine. I found what I think was an eavesdropping device camouflaged as a fuse in the fuse box."

"Huh. Anything else?"

"Yeah, just as I was putting it in my pocket a guy turned up and let himself into the apartment with a key."

"Did you get any information from him?"

"Yeah, he didn't talk much beside the odd grunt. But I have his fingerprints and a blood sample."

"Nice. You couldn't have just asked him a few questions."

"He wasn't real talkative, and he was one tough son of a gun. Anyway, nobody turned up with the ME's report, and I am wondering if this guy was sent in lieu of."

She grunted. "It's possible, I guess. Question: did he look surprised to see you?"

I thought about it, played back the moment where he opened the door and saw me.

"Yeah, it's possible. He wasn't trying to be quiet when he came in. And when he saw me, he hadn't expected it."

"So he wasn't furtive about unlocking and opening the door?"

"No. He just unlocked it and came right in."

"So he was there to get the bug. He wasn't there for you."

I nodded. "Which means the report is still due to be delivered. OK. Listen, I need you to do me a favor."

"Shoot."

"I need you to get this package to Nero. If he can establish the identity of this guy, it might just lead to the leak in DC."

"No problem, we'll run the samples through the Mossad database too. OK, so I am going to make new arrangements for the delivery of the report and I'll get back to you. Where are you now?"

"Right now? In the gardens at the Louvre."

"Stay there. Have an ice cream. I'll get back to you ASAP."

I spent the next half hour wandering among the sixteen gardens that flank the broad, central walkway of the Jardin des Tuileries. It afforded two minutes for each garden, which probably didn't do them justice, though to me it felt like an eternity. Finally, as my belly started telling me it was lunchtime, my cell rang. It was Gallin.

"Where are you?"

"Right where you told me to be. I'm at the Jardin des Tuileries."

She laughed softly. "Your French accent is terrible. OK, so if you walk with your back to the Place du Carrousel toward the Octagonal Pond, just before you get there you'll come to two cafés, one on your right, the other on your left. Am I right?"

"What kind of a question is that, Gallin? You're always right."

"Good. The one on your right is called Pavillon des Tuileries. You are going to go and stand under the tree directly outside the door. A man will approach you and introduce himself as Amin Slimani. He will take it from there."

"Got it."

"And, Mason?

"What are you hoping to find in this report?"

"I don't know. I have nothing right now. I'm looking for anything that will point me toward somebody, who will then lead me back to Washington. A signature, a calling card..." I trailed off.

"OK. Keep me posted."

I found the place she'd described and stood in the shade of the plane tree that was positioned directly outside the café door. Every now and then the smell of a hamburger or a sweet crepe wafted out and tortured my stomach. Another twenty minutes passed and I spotted a man in a faux brown leather jacket approaching me. He was small but his eyebrows were big. In fact they were the biggest eyebrows I had ever seen. They were large, luxuriant and very black. He came right up to me and placed his hand on his heart.

"I am Amin Slimani. You are waiting for me?"

"I think I might be."

"You are interesting about report."

"Walk and talk," I said and started toward the Octagonal Pond. He fell in beside me. I went on, "I would like a copy of the report on Mira Finn's death. She was murdered a few days ago..."

"Yes, I know report. I have report. I am assistant of

medical examiner who makes report. But report is classified."

I let my incredulity show on my face. "*Classified?* Why?"

He shrugged. "I no know. Is make classified by *Brigade de Recherche et d'Intervention.* Copy is take away, but I am already make copy for friend in London. My your friend in London." His words were creating a bewildering maze of grammatically inappropriate junctures. It was the kind of maze where small, white mice died without ever finding the little lever.

I smiled. "Our mutual friend."

"Yes." He nodded deeply, once. "Our mutual friend."

"So how can I get this report? Where is it?"

"Much danger now. Much risk for me."

"I get it. How much?"

We had arrived at the Octagonal Pond and he stood looking into the water. I wondered absently if his eyebrows sometimes obscured his view. He said, "Five thousand dollar American."

"Five grand?"

"Yes, five grand."

"This better be the real thing, Amin. If it's a fake I'll come and find you and shove your head down the can."

"Don't threaten, mister." He said it without much feeling.

I shook my head. "Not threatening, informing. OK, so what next?"

"Tonight you are go to Rue George Thoretton. The number twenty-one B. Big red gate. At twenty-one hour."

"Nine o'clock."

"Yes, nine o'clock. You are bring the money. I give you report."

"How do I know you and half a dozen of your friends aren't going to cut my throat and take my money?"

"No." He grinned an ugly grin. "I am your brother. Also, my your friend in London is come look for us and cut off our balls."

I grunted. "You got that right. OK. I'll be there."

He turned and walked away without saying anything. I watched him a moment. He had a cocky, strutting walk, with his shoulders thrown back too far. It was oddly reminiscent of Christopher Walken. I could hear him in my head: "No! You got the walk...all *wrong!*"

I dismissed the image and decided I didn't trust him as far as I could kick him, and I figured I could kick him pretty far. But I was out of options. Gallin was right, the chances of the report giving me any kind of lead were slim at best, but I could not afford to ignore that chance, however negligible it was.

And as I walked back toward my car, I considered another possibility. If my interest in the report had thrown up a red flag somewhere, and I was walking into a trap that night, well that, however risky it was, was the best lead I had.

I recovered my car and drove north up the Rue du Louvre toward the Hoxton Hotel on the Rue du Sentier. There I checked in, had a martini and a late lunch. Then I went up to my room to have a shower and lie on the bed staring at the ceiling, trying to decide what my best plan of action was that night.

I wasn't crazy about the idea of giving Eyebrows Amin Walken five grand for a document that should have been in the public domain anyhow ("I'm lookin'...at the document, and it's all...*wrong!*"), but I grudgingly decided that if he was on the level, the best thing I could do was pay up and be grateful.

However, my gut was telling me he was not on the level, and one way or another he was going to try and screw me over. He could do that in one of two ways: he could kill me and take the money, or he could sell me to the Russians. My brain said it would be very difficult for the Russians to control French officials that way, especially since Ukraine. My gut told my brain it was talking out of my ass. It was a very organic and slightly surreal conversation.

The main problem I faced was that I was not armed. ODIN had cooperation agreements with many Western governments, and in those countries where you were not allowed to take a weapon in, there were contacts on the ground that could supply you with a weapon once you were there. But I was no longer with ODIN. I was on the run, and contact with ODIN assets or the Company would be as good as suicide.

So I took myself on a shopping expedition, first to a camping shop where I bought six small bottles of propane and a flashlight, and then to a shopping mall where I bought another couple of burners and a roll of large, heavy-duty garden refuse sacks.

I got to the Rue George Thoretton at just before eight o'clock, an hour before I was due, hoping to find the place closed. I was in luck. As I was parking my car, a guy was closing the gate from the outside and locking a padlock on a large chain.

I sat and watched him climb in his truck and drive away.

The place was some kind of workshop. Beyond the gate was a yard, maybe a hundred and twenty feet long and ninety feet across. There were a couple of trucks parked in there, bits of what looked like machinery and old tarps, and along the east side there was a long prefab that looked like some kind of workshop. I couldn't see any CCTV cameras and I couldn't see any warning signs about dogs or alarms.

In my experience, people who have properties which are devoted to criminal activities—a lab, a store for dope or stolen goods, that kind of thing—mostly don't want what they do to be on film, and they sure as hell don't want the cops being alerted if somebody breaks in. They deal with that kind of thing in house.

I climbed out of the car and looked around. The sun was setting and there was a chill in the air. It was quiet and still. This was an industrial area. People didn't live here. They came here to work, and in the evening they went home.

I opened the trunk, pulled out the heavy refuse sack, and made my way to the gate. I had another quick look around, swung the sack over the gate and then pulled myself over. I picked up the sack and ran across the yard to the door of the workshop. Fifteen seconds with the lockpick and the door eased inward. It was very dark. I stepped in, closed the door and switched on the flashlight.

I was in a long, narrow cabin, no more than fifteen feet across. There was a desk and a couple of chairs, stacks of boxes, mostly cartons, and trash everywhere. Working on the principle that people wanting to assert authority or power will gravitate to their desks, I opened the sack, opened the valves on the propane bottles and quickly tied the sack in a tight knot again. This I slid under the desk, out of sight, and made my way back to the car the way I had come.

FOUR

At eight I drove the car the short distance to the gate, got out and stood waiting by the trunk. Fifteen minutes later an old Volkswagen Golf rolled up and Amin Eyebrows leaned out of the passenger window to look at me. There were other guys inside I couldn't make out clearly.

"You bring the money?"

"Did you bring the report?"

"Yes, I bring the report."

"Then I brought the money. Are we going to do this in the middle of the street?"

"No. Wait."

I waited while they parked the car, then watched as Amin climbed out, followed by three guys who had Russian special forces written all over them.

As they approached I jerked my head at the bodyguards. "Who are your friends?"

He nodded and walked to the gate. "Yes, they are my

friends. This is my cousin workshop. We can go inside and have some privacy."

I didn't move. "Hey, Amin." He turned to look at me. "Why have you brought your bodyguards? What's going on?"

I had expected them, and I wasn't surprised to see that they were Russian and not Algerian. But right now it paid dividends to look naïve. He offered me a sickly smile, spread his hands and tilted his head to one side.

"They are just keep me safe. They are friends. We are all brothers. You are my brother. No need for you to worry about them."

I sighed loudly and followed them through the gate and into the yard. It was darker in there, away from the street-lamps, and Eyebrows Amin pulled out a flashlight. We crossed the cold dirt to the steel door of the prefab, he unlocked it and we went inside. One of the Russians closed the door and locked it. He was older than the others, in his thirties, and my gut told me he was the officer, maybe a captain. I moved across the floor, leaving them to gather around the desk.

I addressed Eyebrows, pointing at the Russians. "This has made me very uncomfortable. Let me tell you this, you don't get to see a single cent until I see the report." I pinched my left lapel with forefinger and thumb and pulled open my jacket. "I'm getting my cell." I pulled it out and showed them. "When I see the report and confirm it's authentic, I call and the money gets deposited at the gate."

He simpered and tilted his head again. "Is not necessary to get upset. Just friends helping. No problem."

"Where is the report?"

"Like you, I am careful, I need see money first…"

He shrugged and spread his hands and I said, "Ah, the hell with this," and dialed the number of the cell that was in the black refuse sack. It rang once and everybody frowned and looked back at the desk.

Then there was a loud, ugly, flat bang. The desk jumped and a huge ball of blue and violet flames engulfed Amin and the Russian standing next to him. There were horrible, shrill, hysterical screams. The captain rushed to the aid of his man and I rushed in one long stride to where the other Russian stood gaping at Amin, who was dancing like some bizarre flame daemon. I smacked the Russian backhanded with the flashlight across the back of his neck, and as he swayed I dropped the flashlight and reached in his jacket for the Glock 19 I knew he had there.

I didn't hesitate. After you commit, you can't hesitate. I shot Amin through the head and his dancing fire daemon friend next. The captain had his jacket half off, intending to beat out the flames that were killing his boy. That spoke well of him as a man, but not as an officer. I had the gun steady, pointing at his chest.

"Take off your jacket."

The two bodies lay burning on the floor. There was a sickening stench of burning flesh. He pulled off his jacket, dropped it and held up his hands. He had a shoulder holster and a gun under his left arm. I gestured at it. "Drop the holster."

He did as I said and raised his hands again. I took a couple of steps closer to him, and pointed at the burning bodies.

"You can see I'm serious." He nodded. I aimed the Glock

at his knee. "I am going to shoot you in the knee. Do I need to prove I am serious?"

He went an ugly, waxy color and shook his head. "Not necessary."

"I'm going to ask you some questions. You answer quickly, without hesitation, tell me the truth, and I will let you go home. Hesitate, think too hard, lie to me, and I will shoot you in the knees, first one and then the other. You sure you understand that?"

"I understand."

"You're Russian."

"Yes."

"You're here because I asked about the Mira Finn medical report."

"Yes."

"How is Russia involved with the French government?"

"No," he shook his head, "we are not legal here. We are operating through organized Mafia. We buy Amin. He is our asset, not French government."

"So what is in that report that you don't want me to see?"

He shook his head again. "Nothing. I am not interest in report. I am interest in you. We know you will go for Mira apartment, and then for medical report..."

I frowned and cut him short. "How did you know that?"

He shrugged. "Because you have nothing else. You are escape goat for your bosses. You are lucky you escape from Washington or you are already dead. But when you run, it is obvious you are going to run for Paris. So what you are going to do in Paris? Put advert in *Le Figaro*?" He snorted.

"*Bred sivoy kobyly!* Only you can go to apartment and look at medical report to try and find who is done this to her. Too late we discover you have gone to apartment. But when you kill Ivan and ask about report, then we can make plan to kill you."

"So who is General O'Connor's go-between with Russia?"

He hesitated a fraction of a second; not enough to justify shooting him, but enough to tell me something I had needed to know.

He pulled down the corners of his mouth. "He has Colonel James Gordon, who is Military Intelligence attaché at American Embassy in Madrid."

"Madrid?"

"Yes, secret cooperation between USA and Russian Mafia is happening in Spain, in Marbella. Spanish official very corrupt. When we hear Rusenko is coming through Paris, is easy to send units here to intercept him."

"You have him?"

He took three whole seconds to answer. "No."

"You know where he is?"

"No. He is gone. We are watching embassy, but I think is scared to go to embassy."

He was working hard to conceal the smile, but he was failing.

"What's the joke?"

"You need find him and catch him. We don't need catch him or find him. It is enough we stop you."

I frowned, trying to read him. "What are you talking about?"

He narrowed his eyes. "You don't know... *Yebat*

Kalatit!" Suddenly he laughed. "You don't know! You don't know why Rusenko is so important. You don't know why you are going to die."

The flames were guttering on the two charred bodies and the narrow room was filling with an acrid, nauseating stench. I tried to ignore it, blinking the stinging smoke from my eyes.

"But you are going to tell me, or I am going to start plugging holes in your joints."

"Yes, I will tell you. You have maybe thirty-six, maybe forty-eight hours to find Rusenko. I don't know exact hours. But when time is pass, then it is too late. Then it is game over." He started laughing again. I was blinking hard. "You eyes hurting, Mr. Mason? No problem, I have the remedy!"

I fired too late. He lunged at me, levered the barrel up and slammed the heel of his hand into my wrist. He turned the weapon on me, but he was too close. I was practically blind, but I stepped closer to him, gripped his wrist and forearm and smashed my instep into his balls. His eyes rolled up in his head and his knees bent. I snatched the weapon back and with tears streaming down my face, I shot him and the guy whose gun I'd stolen in the head.

Now it was game over.

I wrenched open the door, stumbled out of the prefab into the cold night and stood vomiting and coughing against the wall. The upside was that it produced enough tears to clear my eyes. The downside was that I had left enough DNA to keep every lab in Paris busy for a week.

I did my best to contaminate the sample by mixing it with samples from inside, then killed the lights and made my way back to the car. I climbed in, fired up the engine, and spent the next half hour driving aimlessly through the suburbs, seeing nothing but the two men enveloped in flames, screaming pitifully; and the man I'd come to think of as the captain sneering at me: *"You have maybe thirty-six, maybe forty-eight hours to find Rusenko. I don't know exact hours. But when time is pass, then it is too late. Then it is game over."*

Thirty-six hours, maybe forty-eight. Why those numbers? Rusenko was a scientist. He had information of interest to the USA, but neither Nero nor O'Connor, nor the president for that matter, had said anything about time limits. What would happen in thirty-six or forty-eight hours? Would Rusenko die?

Streetlamps and headlamps pulsed in the dark, like a slow heartbeat filling the cab with dull light, then passing on in a steady, rhythmic flow. Shops flowed past, silent but illuminated, restaurants, cafés, bistros—and people, thousands of people, laughing, talking, drinking, confident in the immutable nature of their lives.

Thirty-six to forty-eight hours.

Game over.

Why had he laughed? What was it about my ignorance that had amused him?

I had no answers for my questions, but I knew, beyond the faintest shadow of a doubt, that I had to find Rusenko— now.

What the CIA and ODIN could not do, not to mention the Russian SVR, with all their resources, I had to do in the next few hours. I didn't know if Rusenko was still in the country. More than that, even if he was, I didn't even know where to start looking.

I came to a bridge and was suddenly aware of the Eiffel Tower looming vast into the night sky. And that somehow triggered something else the captain had said: "So what you are going to do in Paris? Put advert in *Le Figaro*?"

And suddenly I was acutely aware that we were back in the Cold War. Russia was attempting to recreate the Soviet Union, China was making menacing noises about Taiwan, and the West, reeling from this sudden, unexpected turn of events, was scrambling to shore up its defenses. And at the heart of it all was the arms race again. But this time it was not just a case of stockpiling more nuclear missiles than could ever be used. This time it was the worst nightmares of the '60s, '70s and '80s made flesh. This time there were no Russian pragmatists in the Kremlin rattling sabers. What we had this time was a paranoid megalomaniac who was driving himself into a psychotic break.

But there was something else tickling at the back of my mind. Something about the Cold War, and what the Russian captain had said. So what was I going to do in Paris? he'd asked. Put an advert in *Le Figaro*?

And that had been, of course, an integral part of spy craft during the Cold War, using the classified columns of leading newspapers to send and receive coded messages. *Le Figaro* was the paper with the widest circulation in France. Was it worth a try? I had nothing to lose, after all, and nothing else I *could* try.

So I made my way back to the hotel and went online to search for *Le Figaro* classified ads. When I'd found them I sat staring at the screen and thinking. Eventually I typed.

Doctor, we have less than forty-eight hours to save the world. Nanny is not here, but I'd like to help. We are all puppets in the fields of the god of war. If we are at that stage, let's hope it's not too late for a new morning.

I SAT STARING at the message with a sinking feeling of despair. Even in the very unlikely event that Rusenko would think of checking the classified ads in *Le Figaro*, the chances of his seeing the add, much less realizing it was meant for him, were one in a million.

On the other hand, right then, I could not think of another option save roaming the streets hoping to see him in some vagrant shelter. I entered my card details and clicked send. After that I showered and went down to the bar for a stiff drink. It was while I was in the corner, easing my bruised limbs and sipping a large whiskey, that one of my burners rang. The screen told me it was Gallin.

I answered and said, "I should have binned this one already."

"I'm guessing you only used it to call me?"

"Yes—"

"Then you are still within safe parameters. Destroy it after this call."

"Yes sir."

"Update me."

"I can't. I'm in a bar. But I ran into a captain in the Russian army. Well, I assumed he was a captain. And he thought it was very amusing that I didn't realize I had only between thirty-six and forty-eight hours to get the job done."

She was quiet for so long I thought she'd walked away from the phone.

"Thirty-six to forty-eight hours? So what happens if you find him before thirty-six hours?"

"Yeah. I think that's something Nero never shared with me. I know he's a scientist who was engaged in military projects. I got the impression it was biological warfare, but Nero was always cagey about it."

"How are you going to find him?"

"That's what the whiskey and I were discussing when you interrupted us. We were trying to work out what steps to take next. So far I have put a classified ad in *Le Figaro*. I know it sounds stupid but, aside from the fact that I couldn't think of anything else, I also figured he would be thinking the same as me. And I remembered also that Nero had said Rusenko was a fan of Le Carré, Len Deighton and cryptic crosswords. So he might figure, if his chaperone is still in Paris, how does he contact him…?"

I trailed off, feeling I was trying too hard to justify what I'd done. She surprised me by saying, "That's good. We still use that a lot too. What does it say?"

"Doctor, we have only thirty-six hours to save the world. Nanny is not here, but I'd like to help. We are all puppets in the fields of the god of war. If we are at that stage, let's hope it's not too late for a new morning."

"OK, you let him know Mira is dead but you're here, and you want to meet him at the Champs de Mars puppet theater in the morning."

"Really? You got that?"

Yeah, I also like Le Carré, Len Deighton and cryptic crosswords. It's good. But Mason, you have almost zero resources. If that doesn't work out, how the hell are you going to make contact?"

I nodded and sighed. "I know, and the last thing I need is for him to panic and contact the US Embassy. Chances are he would get swallowed up by the CIA and the military-industrial complex, and would never again see the light of day. This captain also mentioned a Colonel James Gordon, an attaché at the US Embassy in Madrid. You heard of him?"

"No. I'll make inquiries. Is he in O'Connor's pay?"

I hesitated. "That was the general gist of it, yeah."

"Thirty-six to forty-eight hours..."

"A little less than that now."

"OK, listen, tell the concierge you are expecting your wife in the early hours of the morning. I'll get the first flight out."

I hung up and smiled. Not a bad end to a crap day.

FIVE

She arrived at four AM. I had my hand on the stolen Glock under my pillow as she crept into the room. I watched her undress in the faint light from the window, and climb into bed beside me. When she was lying down I whispered, "I almost shot you."

"I know, I heard your breathing change. I figured I was safe once I started taking my clothes off."

"Does this represent a change in our relationship?"

"Shut up and go to sleep."

But she put her head on my shoulder and I smelt her hair. It was a special moment.

By seven AM we were up, showered and breakfasted, and on our way to the Eiffel Tower. We found a parking space on the Rue de Belgrade in the abundant shade of trees I could not identify, and walked the short distance to the Monument to the Rights of Man at the entrance to the Champs de Mars.

Gallin took a moment to stop in front of the monument, sigh and shake her head. "They have a genius for being weird," she said. I didn't say anything, so she looked at me and added, in case I hadn't got it, "The French. 'Alors, Pierre.'" She started acting out a weird scenario in her head, in a heavy French accent. "Ah sought we could build a monument to zee rights of man. Where shall we put it? Aha! Voila! Ah know! We can put it in zee Champs de Mars, where we make tribute to zee god of war!"

"Done?"

"Yeah." We started walking again, along the curving paths, through the trees toward the puppet theater. "Have you seen their cars, though?" she insisted. "They make weird cars. I mean, a car with an arse! Seriously? They love to be weird."

After four or five minutes of examples of weird things the French did, which included, "Voila, Yvette! A slimy slug in a shell, why don't we boil it and eat it?" we came by and by to the *Marionnettes du Champs de Mars*, a cute, covered puppet theater, painted green and nestled among trees on a large patch of lawn. It was closed. It was still early and there was barely a person in sight. There was a large plane tree outside the entrance, and beside it a green park bench. I sat and Gallin sat beside me.

"You think I should go?"

"No. I don't want to spook him by having somebody hidden who shows up later. And two of us makes better cover."

"I guess we have to be prepared for the possibility that he did not check the classified ads."

"That's what I said yesterday. You said it was a good plan."

"I know. I'm just saying. What's our plan if he doesn't show? We now have just twenty-four to thirty-six hours."

I made a minute study of the sky, and the trees that stood between me and it. No magical solutions sprang out at me.

"Is this an issue that might be of the remotest interest to Mossad?"

"I asked my father, and he said yes, it would be of the remotest interest to Mossad. In as much as it could affect the balance of power between Russia and the USA, and so weaken America's support for Israel. Israel likes a strong America."

I sighed. "We need resources to search the city. Hell, we don't know if he's even in Paris anymore."

She leaned her elbows on her knees and stared at the yellow earth between her feet. "He said we couldn't devote time or resources to helping you find Rusenko. The most he could do for the moment was give me some leave of absence, and he wanted me to point out that doing so could harm our relationship with the Pentagon and the CIA."

"I appreciate it."

A desultory scattering of people had entered the park, looking sleepy in the early morning chill, hands in pockets, shoulders hunched. Nobody approached the small, green theater.

"I guess I'll have to kill Alex Mason."

She frowned at me. "What are you talking about?"

"If we can't find Rusenko, I'll have to die. You'll have to identify the body. And I'll have to reincarnate in Brazil, or India. It's a shame. I never really liked Brazil or India as places to live."

She sighed and looked away. "I don't want to agree with you, but I think you might be right, Mason. We had one shot. We took it and we struck water."

"Unless we go to Madrid and find Colonel James Gordon."

She laughed out loud. "Well, I guess if you have run out of things to lose, you could try that."

I noticed a man in a shabby raincoat approaching. He had sallow, olive skin, a large, domed head that was bald on top and long, wispy dark hair flowing down from just above his ears. He had a languid, loping walk and strange, penetrating dark eyes which he kept trained on us as he approached.

"Good morning," he said, still some distance away. The accent was from India, not Russia, and had the exquisite resonance and enunciation of the Brahmin.

"Good morning."

"Not quite April, but still a lovely time in Paris."

"It sure is."

"Sometimes," he said, coming to a halt a few feet from me and addressing Gallin, "I postpone my breakfast so that I can take an early morning stroll and stop somewhere for some coffee and brioche. You are visiting Paris?"

Gallin didn't answer so I said, "Just for a few days."

He sighed with exaggerated sadness and shrugged his shabby shoulders. "It is not the Paris of legend anymore, I am afraid. The Paris of the *fauve* movement, or even of Albert Camus or Jean-Paul Sartre," he pronounced the names with a flawless French accent, "oh, dear me, no. Today it is Euro-Paris, a standardized city of immigrants, refugees and racial tension, where the French feel as dispossessed and marginalized as do the ethnic minorities. But it is still a very beautiful city." He regarded us both for a moment and added, "I find people usually come to Paris searching for something."

"Searching for what?"

He pushed out his bottom lip. "Oh, goodness me, it might be love, romance, freedom…"

I smiled and gave a small chuckle. "If one were searching for freedom, he might as well put an ad in the classified columns of *Le Figaro*."

He closed his eyes and leaned forward as he laughed silently. "Oh, indeed! That would not be a bad plan. But then one might find something completely unexpected, like an Indian professor of quantum physics, instead of a Russian professor of cosmology."

"You know him?"

He shambled over and sat next to me on the park bench. Gallin leaned against the plane tree and watched us both, glancing periodically up and down the path.

"Gosh yes, I have known him for many years. We have corresponded a great deal, and he has often visited me in Paris."

"He is a dangerous person to know at the moment."

"Yes, but he is even more dangerous to ignore. Besides, I have had my visits from the French police and from the Russian Mafia. I convinced them I was the last person on Earth he would come to, precisely because everybody knows we are friends. And I promised I would let them know the moment I heard from him."

Gallin spoke for the first time. "Who saw the ad, you or him?"

He smiled at her for a good five seconds before answering. "He did, and he pointed it out to me."

"Is he staying with you?"

"Forgive me, miss, but who are you?"

She looked at me. I said, "You ask her but you don't ask me?"

"Yes, indeed. In one of their last conversations, just before he came to Paris, Mira told him that she had an uncomfortable feeling of uncertainty. She could not identify exactly why, but she had an intuition that something was wrong. And so she told our mutual friend that if things went 'arse over tit,' as she put it, they would send a man for him, and she described you quite accurately. She said he would be like a tall, elegant King Kong."

Gallin laughed. "She nailed you, pal."

"Yeah, so, Dr...?"

"Raj Patel, associate professor of quantum physics at the Sorbonne. I invite you to check on me, but I remind you that we are desperately short of time."

Before he'd finished talking Gallin had taken a picture of him and was walking away, talking into her cell.

"We are short of time, why?"

"You don't know?" He looked faintly surprised.

"I was asked the same question last night. Unfortunately the Russian officer who asked me didn't live long enough to tell me."

"Oh, dear. Mira was not exaggerating, then."

I smiled. "Elegant might be a bit of an exaggeration. What happens in twenty-four to thirty-six hours if I don't find Dr. Rusenko, Dr. Patel?"

"Oh, Raj, please. Well, it is reassuring to me that you

don't know, because all the people who want Peter—that is, Dr. Rusenko—dead *know* what will happen. But, before we start sharing information, I should like to know who your friend is. Also, I am not very clear *on whose behalf* you are here to get Peter."

I thought about how to answer him. I decided I was probably satisfied he was who he said he was, and also that I was pretty much out of options: I had to tell him what he needed to know if he was going to help us. I nodded and shrugged.

"I'm the fall guy. There's a leak in DC. Somebody informed the Russians that Dr. Rusenko was coming to Paris, and that Mira was going to be his nanny. The leak could have been one of four men. Three of them were untouchable, above the law. So I took the fall. My boss told me to run, come to Paris, rescue Dr. Rusenko and find the leak."

He nodded a lot. "That was what Mira was sensing then."

"I'd say so." I nodded toward Gallin, who was walking back toward us. "She is Israeli, a good friend on leave of absence while she helps me out."

"I see, I see. She is very able."

Gallin nodded and smiled at Dr. Patel. "Checks out. So what's next?"

"I will talk to Peter and put him up to speed. If he is agreeable, I will arrange a meeting. How you get him from Paris to Washington is up to you, I'm afraid."

"We'll take care of that. But now it is my turn to remind you, Doctor, that we are very short of time, and I still don't know why."

He drew breath, hesitated and then shook his head. "Dear me, I wish I could tell you, but it is best if it comes from him. All I can say is that it is very urgent that he makes contact with the *right* people in Washington, you understand. The *right* people. If he doesn't, if it is too late, very bad things will happen."

"If it is that bad, that urgent, why can't you tell us?"

He held my eye for a long moment. "Because only he knows precisely what the time frame is, and what precisely you need to know." He stood. "How can I contact you?"

I pulled an unused burner from my pocket and activated it. I gave him the number. "You are the only person who has this number now."

"I have an eidetic memory. I will not forget."

And with that he walked away, across the fields of Mars, France's monument to war. I thought about that for a moment as I sat on the bench and watched his angular, scruffy figure disappear. Maybe the French were weird after all, like Gallin had said. If there was one country in the world you'd think wouldn't want a monument to war, it would be France. I smiled to myself: a monument to war incorporating the Rights of Man and a puppet theater. Weird, I thought. Things are rarely what they seem.

Gallin watched him walk away too, until he was lost among the trees. When he was gone she turned to me.

"What do you make of it?"

"When I ask my gut, it goes Italian on me. It shrugs and spreads its hands and says, 'You askin' me? What do I know?' I ask my brain and it tells me, if he was working for the Russians, we would have been quietly ambushed and killed here this morning." I gave my head a small twitch. "I think he's on the level. What did you get?"

"He *is* an associate professor of physics at the Sorbonne. That much they were able to confirm. I have one of the guys looking into him to see if we can confirm his friendship with Rusenko. Also, while I remember, we drop off your DNA and prints samples at the Israeli Embassy."

I nodded. "Good." Then I screwed up my face and said, "Cosmology..."

"I know." She sat beside me. "It does not scream biological warfare, does it?"

"I see the To The Stars Academy looming, with Luis Elizondo in tow and news of the return of Oumuamua."

"What are you talking about, Mason?"

"Cosmology. What the hell has cosmology got to do with national security and the conflict between Russia and NATO?"

Her cell rang and she reached in her pocket for it.

"Yeah."

She was silent for a while then said, "*Toda*," and hung up.

"What?"

"We were aware of Dr. Raj Patel, we have been for quite a time, because as a Brahmin he has very strong views on Islam. He has been a friend of Rusenko's for many years. They have collaborated on numerous occasions in the field of space telescopes, laser applications and theoretical faster-than-light interstellar travel."

I groaned. "Jesus..."

"I think you're missing the point, Mason."

I looked at her and she held my eye. "Oh," I said as it dawned on me. "Oh, Jesus! Thirty-six hours..."

She shook her head. "He said he didn't know the timeframe."

"Gallin, we have to trust that he will contact us with sufficient time. Meanwhile, we need to come up with a way out of France and back to the USA that is fast. We have absolutely no time to spare."

"OK, we need to get lost for a few hours. Correction: you need to get lost for a while. I need to go and talk to some people. Drop me on Matignon and Rabelais, go get anything you might need from the hotel, get a cab and go to the Market Restaurant."

"You going to tell me why I am going to do all these things?"

"I'll explain on the way to the car."

She explained on the way to the car. It wasn't a long walk, but it wasn't a complicated explanation, either. It made sense and it would probably work. It would probably work if we were right and Dr. Patel was Rusenko's long-time friend. It would probably work if he hadn't been bought or threatened. And it might work if, given all the above, he contacted us in time to make it happen. It was a lot of *ifs*, but *ifs* were all we had right then, so we'd have to make the most of it.

I dropped her at the corner of Avenue Matignon and Rue Rabelais and watched her walk quickly away through the crowds toward the Israeli Embassy. I tried to remember what I knew about Rabelais. It was a phrase of his that Crowley had borrowed, "Do as thou wilt shall be all of the law."

I pulled away and headed back toward the hotel. We had become so accustomed to the stable, orderly, market-driven society we'd inhabited in the West since the end of the Second World War, that we had lost touch with the fact there were those out there in the world who lived by a different code: Crowley's code, Rabelais' code—do as thou wilt shall be *all* of the law.

SIX

I DIDN'T PAY THE BILL AT THE HOTEL. I'D DO THAT by phone, later. I left all our luggage but took the essentials like passports, driver's licenses, cash, et cetera—basically what was in the safe. Then I left the car at the hotel and took a cab to the Market Restaurant, around the corner from the Israeli Embassy. It was a little early for lunch, so I sat at a table in the corner and ordered myself a martini. Gallin showed up fifteen minutes later, alone.

I stood and pulled out her chair as she sat.

"I talked to the office in Tel Aviv. We called Dad and had a conference."

"And."

"They figure maybe this could be important, so they are willing to give us a hand."

"What about their relationship with the company? There could be fallout from being seen to help a fugitive."

"Keep your voice down and don't use words like that. That is understood and they have *no idea* they are helping you." She labored the words, indicating they were not true. "If it hits the fan, you and me will be getting plastic surgery in Brazil together."

"Great. Something to look forward to. So exactly how can they help?"

"Rough outline—we will have to improvise and adapt as the situation develops. But basically, when we get the call we arrange a meet. We explain to Peter what's going to happen next and I call my pals. They collect him and from that point on he is under Israeli protection. I contact Nero directly and either we meet in DC or we meet in Paris or..." She shrugged.

I thought it through, nodding. "That is an almost perfect plan."

"It's almost perfect because it is only part of the plan. I kept the part you wouldn't like till last."

"Let me guess. You get to hand over the package and I get to go and look for Colonel James Gordon."

"It's the only way to do it. There is simply no time for anything else. We bring him in together and it helps your case, but it doesn't clear you and it does not expose the rot in DC. You need your witness."

"You're right."

The waiter came to take our order and my cell rang.

"Yeah."

"Good afternoon. This is Dr. Patel. I wonder if you are very busy."

"Not at all."

"Would this be a convenient time to meet?"

"Perfect." I gestured with my eyes that Gallin should pay for my martini and stood. "Where would be convenient?"

We left the waiter muttering French obscenities and stepped out into the midday sun. There was an illegally parked Ford Fiesta with diplomatic plates just across from the entrance. The lights bleeped and Gallin climbed in behind the wheel. Dr. Patel was saying, "You will please take the N3 to the town of Claye, about fifteen or sixteen miles northeast of Paris."

I put the phone on speaker and told Gallin, "Fifteen or sixteen miles northeast of Paris on the N3, town called Claye."

She pulled out into the traffic, glancing over her shoulder and causing a chorus of horns and obscenities. She muttered a few of her own and we accelerated up toward the Champs Elysées to take the Périphérique at the vast circus at the Place de la Port Maillot. She didn't drop below fifty, and taught that little Fiesta things Ford never intended it to know.

While we swerved in and out of traffic, Dr. Patel kept talking.

"When you arrive at Claye, you'll find there is a Carrefour hypermarket at the very entrance to the town, on your left-hand side. And immediately afterwards there is a frightfully confusing intersection, like spaghetti. What you want to do then is come off so that you are going north on the D212, for Soissons. Almost immediately you will come to a roundabout," here he giggled, "goodness! I think you Americans call them circuses. Go straight across. Straight across! And after maybe a quarter of a mile, you will come to a petrol station. A gas station to you. There you pull in and you will find it is one of the few petrol stations left that still has a public pay phone, on the wall outside."

"A pay phone."

"Be there in twenty minutes. I will call you at that number. Answer it and I will tell you where to go from there."

Gallin snapped, "We are short of time, Dr. Patel."

"But I must minimize risk, dear lady."

The traffic was heavy, but Gallin drove like a thing demented and we got to the gas station with four minutes to spare. So while Gallin filled the tank and paid, I leaned by the phone and waited. It rang on the dot and I snatched the receiver.

"Yeah."

"Oh, splendid, splendid. That is very good indeed. Now, I am ninety-nine percent sure this telephone is not bugged, so I feel somewhat more secure."

"That's great. What do you want us to do now, Doctor?"

"Come out of the petrol station and head north along the D212 until you come to the junction with the N2. There you will turn right—east—and follow the N2 as far as Le Plessis-Belleville. There you take the N330 north. At Ermenonville you will enter the forest of that name, and you will continue along the N330, moving ever north and east, until deep in the woods you come to the junction with the D126. There you turn left, south and west, for half a mile, and finally, on the right, you will come to my house. You can't miss it. It is set back from the road a little behind cypress trees. You will be very welcome there. Have you retained all of that?"

"I've got it."

I hung up and we climbed back in the car, and after half

an hour of beautiful French fields in spring, and dense pine forests, we finally came to an old farmhouse you could just make out through a hedge of thuja trees. The gate was down a dirt track and had been left open. We pulled in and saw that the house stood in about two acres of land, screened on all sides by a wall of cypress trees. I climbed out and closed the gate, and we followed a gravel path down to an old, two-storey stone building with a gabled, slate roof. The walls were flanked by flowerbeds, and honeysuckle had climbed partway over a wooden porch over the front door.

While Gallin parked the car out of sight of the road, I pressed the button in the large, brass plate beside the door. It was opened after a couple of minutes by Dr. Patel, who greeted us like we'd come to spend the weekend.

"You made it, splendid. My instructions were not too confusing. Goodness yes, that is splendid." He ushered us through the door and led the way down a narrow passage with bare wooden floors that creaked underfoot. "Peter is in the garden at the back of the house. We were just having a little luncheon. I hope you'll join us."

We passed through a stone-flagged kitchen with lots of brightly colored iron pots and a gigantic wooden dresser. It was the sort of kitchen favored by Ivy League academics who simply love Europe. There was even a string of onions and a string of garlic hanging from the side. It was very wholesome.

We followed Dr. Patel out through the kitchen door into a walled garden which was about thirty feet square. The walls were redbrick and largely obscured by fruit trees, mainly apples and cherries, and a couple of lemon trees which were convenient for the evening gin and tonics. The rest of the area was taken up by herb bushes, and a flagged area outside the kitchen. There they had set up a large, wooden farmhouse table laden with cheese, ham, a huge earthenware bowl of complicated salad and a couple of crusty baguettes. There were also a couple of bottles of white wine stuck in a bucket of ice. Nero would have approved.

At the head of the table was a man in his sixties. He got to his feet as we emerged from the kitchen. He was tall and angular, with considerable elbows and large feet. He had hair he clearly didn't think about a lot, and bright eyes that seemed to be permanently amused.

He embraced us like we were long-lost friends, lingering a little longer than was strictly necessary over Gallin. When he was done, he quite literally begged us to join them.

"Please, I beg you, join us for lunch. Did you eat? This is very good, and Raj has wonderful cellar. Wine is superb."

The places were already set so we pulled out chairs and sat.

"Dr. Rusenko—"

"Peter, please. You have suffered so much because of me, least I can do is offer my friendship. I feel..." He closed his eyes and shook his head, pounding his chest with his old fist. "I feel my heart is going to break, poor Mira, and now you. Is too bad, too bad."

I started again. "Peter, there will be time later to deal with the pain and the grief, but right now we have to be very practical. I was told last night by a Russian paramilitary that we had thirty-six to forty-eight hours to find you. I don't know what he was talking about, but I can tell you right now that it worries me." I gestured at Dr. Patel. "And Dr. Patel told me this morning that we now had twenty-four hours. I need to know, right now, what happens in twenty-four hours. And I also need to get you to Washington, and I am really not sure we have time for lunch."

Rusenko nodded slowly with his eyes closed while I was speaking. When I had finished he opened his eyes and shrugged.

"If we have no *time* for lunch, my friend, it makes no difference whether we have or not, because there is nothing we can do. But," he smiled at Gallin, "I think we have an hour while we wait for our friends from the Mossad to arrive. Am I mistaken?"

Gallin shook her head while she helped herself to the complicated salad, which included rice and chickpeas as well as avocado and tuna.

"No, you're not," she said, "but we don't want to get too comfortable either. We need you to tell us exactly what happens in twenty-four or thirty-six hours if we don't get you to DC."

The humor drained out of his face. There was suddenly a great stillness about the garden. I became acutely aware of the birds chirruping in the trees, of the sporadic breeze moving the leaves in the spring sunshine. Rusenko sighed and sagged back in his chair, waving a hand beside his ear like he was trying to silence his nagging ghosts.

"Yah!" he said, "I am cosmologist." He looked up at the sky, smiling suddenly. "Cosmologist!" he repeated in a high squeak. "My calling, my passion, is always to discover how the universe is working." He turned to Gallin with wide eyes, full of childlike glee. "Are molecules alive? Why life only appears at cellular level? What makes flowers grow? *How do flowers know how to grow?* Are flowers same here and on Proxima B? Does life in the universe follow same patterns everywhere? Same as non-living things do? These and so many, many more questions I am asking since I am small boy."

The animation drained from his face as suddenly as it had arrived, and he sagged back once more and grunted.

"But Putin is crazy bastard. He is calling me to presidential office and he is telling me, 'I know you work a lot with lasers, a lot. Very much. You use lasers for many wonderful things, I know...'" He jabbed his finger at me, punctuating his words. "'I *know* you are working *lot* with satellites, and you have help *design* satellites. So now I am make you *head of project* to design very special satellite with lasers.' He say to me, 'I call this satellite, Shadow of Death.' I say to him, 'Shadow of Death? What is Shadow of Death satellite?'"

He sat nodding for a moment, staring first left and then right at nothing in particular. Then he shook his head.

"'Shadow of Death satellite,'" he tell me, "'is satellite with stealth capability, undetectable to radar, and with paint which is absorbing light, so it does not reflect. It is a satellite which is invisible. It is equipped with laser targeting which is —" He sat forward and raised his finger above his head. "— which is *programmable in advance*; and this satellite, Shadow of Death, can carry arsenal of *nuclear weapons!* Because this satellite is the size of a space station. Very, very few people in the world know that we are making this weapon." He lifted his index again. "Putin," he raised his thumb, "me," his middle finger, "Nero," he dropped his hand on the table, "two Russian generals chief of staff, General O'Connor and the president of United States. And now you three. But that we have finish and launch it? Putin, me and General O'Connor, I think."

I had gone very cold and I could feel the hair on my arms prickling. I glanced at Gallin and saw that she was frozen with a fork halfway to her mouth. I asked:

"How many missiles can this satellite deploy?"

"New York, San Francisco, Los Angeles and Washington DC, also London, Brussels, Berlin and Paris," he paused, "eight cities, three times. Twenty-four missiles."

Gallin expostulated, "*Three times!* That's insane! Not even Putin is that crazy!"

"Ha! Believe me, dear lady, Putin is that crazy. You in the West do not understand! You do not understand Middle East and you do not understand the East! But you *must* understand! If West is going to survive, *you must understand!*"

He paused to shake his head again. The birds twittered and the leaves rustled in the gentle sunshine.

Rusenko went on. "Listen to me. We live in time where more and more countries are governed not by governments, but by men. Like in old times. And if you are not crazy when you take the throne, you will for sure be crazy if, after ten years, you have not left! Because personal political power *make you crazy!*"

I interrupted. "Please, let's cut to the chase. When exactly is the launch programmed for...?"

Rusenko looked at Dr. Patel, who closed his eyes and nodded.

"We still have approximately thirty-six hours. He has launch window of twelve hours to strike all cities simultaneously. So, between thirty-six and forty-eight. Final launch is up to him."

He paused, staring at his hands on the old wooden table. "You must understand—the missiles are small, only eight or nine feet long. And once they are launched they are impossible to detect. Initially they are fired like bullet from gun. *Bang!* No engines. Engines are kick in only in last ten miles, and then rockets go hypersonic. They will destroy New York completely, District of Columbia and Virginia—White House, Capitol, Pentagon, CIA, FBI...," he was shaking his head, "will destroy completely financial district of Los Angeles and San Francisco, including Silicon Valley. They will take out City of London, completely destroy Brussels, and annihilate Berlin and Paris. By evening of that day, Western civilization will not exist."

The words hung in the fresh spring air, unreal, like radioactive insanity raining invisible out of a perfect blue sky.

My voice seemed loud and jarring when I spoke. "So how do we stop it? There must be some way to stop it!"

He nodded for a moment, then gave a shrug that seemed to say, *perhaps.*

"They make it very clear to me when they make me head of project, if I do not collaborate, they will torture my wife and my children. I agree and I immediately start, with my friend Raj, to plan escape and disappearance of my wife and children. That happened finally last month. That is when I contact Pentagon and they connect me with General O'Connor. And he is making arrangements for me to escape to USA. At this time I believe Kremlin knows nothing."

He stopped suddenly and sat thinking in silence, staring at his glass of golden wine on the rough, wooden table.

"So, now, all we need is for me to give coordinates, launch codes and communication protocols to NSA, and they will locate and neutralize satellite."

I said, "But somebody told the Kremlin."

"Exactly, so now I am assume codes and the protocols have been changed. Coordinates must stay constant. So I think only hope is to take out satellite with a laser. I think USA has big laser in Area 51."

"What about a missile?"

He shook his head. "No. It will detect missile and shoot it down with laser."

"And do you know how to find the satellite?"

"Probably."

"Jesus Christ!"

"I think he will not help you. Me? Maybe I can help you."

Gallin pulled her cell from her pocket and dialed. She stood and moved away from the table toward the fruit trees with the phone to her ear. After a moment I heard her say: "It's worse than we thought. A lot worse. I need a chopper at my location ten minutes ago. We need to get this man and his colleague to DC in the next few hours. You had better have a jet standing by. If we don't get him to ODIN today we are *all* as screwed as a dime whore during shore leave."

I pulled my last burner from my pocket and activated it. From memory I dialed in Nero's private number. His voice was frowning when he answered.

"Who is this? How did you get this number?"

"It's me. Don't talk. Listen. Russia is planning satellite-launched nuclear strikes on DC, New York, San Francisco and Los Angeles, as well as London, Brussels, Paris and Berlin, in anything between thirty-six and forty-eight hours." I heard a splutter, ignored it and moved on. "I'm sending you the man who can stop them—the man you sent me to get, and his colleague. He will be arriving care of the Israeli diplomatic bag in the next few hours. But listen to me very carefully, sir. He cannot go to DC. The White House is leaking like a colander. Maybe the Pentagon too. So you'd better talk directly to Groom Lake, have the flight sent directly there, and talk to them about using lasers. The satellite cannot be stopped. It must be destroyed. But it is imperative you cut the White House and the Pentagon out of this until it's over."

He was very quiet for a moment. Then, "I see. What about you?"

"I am going to clear my name, sir."

SEVEN

Within the half hour an Airbus H155 came thundering over the forest, silencing the birds, making the trees bow and toss and knocking over the glasses of white wine that still stood on the table. Gallin got to her feet and gestured to the hovering chopper to land in the grounds of the house. The pilot saluted and he began to descend out of view behind the house. I turned to Rusenko and Patel.

"You stay here. We'll go check these are who we think they are."

They both looked at me with sad eyes and said nothing. Gallin and I pulled our weapons and made for the front door. She went out first because she said they were her people. I tried to explain that the problem would be if they were *not* her people. She wasn't listening. She pulled open the door with her piece held out in front of her and went out. I was right behind her.

The pilot and his pal had jumped down from the idling chopper, and when they saw Gallin with her Sig pointed at them they started to laugh. The pilot shouted, "We love you too, Aila! This is the Gallin welcome."

His pal shouted, "Save it for the Ayatollah, Aila."

She holstered her piece and I followed suit. Next thing they were giving each other manly handshakes and slapping each other's shoulders. "Ethan, Paul," she pointed at me and said, "this guy is not here."

The pilot laughed again. "Don't take it personal. She does that to all the guys."

There was more laughing. Gallin cut in, addressing the pilot.

"OK, Ethan, these are your instructions. You take the package from here to the Aérolithe airfield, six miles southeast from here, just north of Le Plessis-Belleville."

The pilot nodded. "I know where it is."

"There will be a Gulfstream G650 waiting for you. You know the pilot, Daniel—" She gave him a knowing look and he smiled. "Ah, OK."

"He will have Moshe and Dave with him. Hand over to them and only them. Anybody tries to take the package you kill them, and you die before you let go of them. I am serious."

"Got it. Where's the package?"

She looked at me. I smiled. "I guess I am here after all."

I went and called the doctors. They both came out with rucksacks, looking bizarrely like very old children off for their first day at school. Dr. Patel was shaking his head and grumbling.

"It really seems quite unnecessary. There will be questions asked at the university. How am I to explain? It is really too much…"

I assured him we'd take care of the university and watched them both clamber into the chopper. Paul climbed in too and Ethan hung around with his door open. I turned to Gallin. "Call me when you're safely in the jet and in the air."

Her eyes flicked over my face, like it had somehow gone wrong and she didn't like it anymore. "What?"

"When you're in the plane, at Le Plessis-Belleville, and you have taken off," I showed her what taken off was with my hand, "call me. Let me know..."

"Yeah, yeah. I understood the words, Mason. It was 'what' like, 'What are you talking about?' I am not going to the States. I'm here with you."

I shook my head. "No, what you've done so far can be justified because you are bringing Rusenko in, but you can't be seen to be assisting a fugitive..."

"Yadda yadda yadda yadda." She started flapping her hand in my face. "Save your hill of beans speech for some Swedish bimbo who gives a damn. This ain't *Casablanca*, chum."

She waved at Ethan and gave him the thumbs up. He pulled himself in, slammed the door and within seconds the downdraft was flattening the grass around us and making the trees toss and twist. Instinctively we ducked and retreated toward the house, and next thing the chopper was a black stencil against the blue sky, tilting and veering away to the south.

When it had gone I turned and looked at her. There was humor in her eyes, but not in mine. "You shouldn't have done that, Gallin. I'm not just a fugitive from the law. I have agents from the Russian SVR hunting me to kill me, and I probably also have agents from several US agencies hunting for me. CIA, Military Intelligence..."

"Yeah."

"And I have no backup, Gallin. ODIN has washed its hands of me. I have no resources."

She was watching me with her mouth slightly open. "Uh-huh."

"You can't be involved with me, Gallin."

"You done?" I didn't say anything so she nodded for me. "Right, for some reason I don't understand my dad likes you. He says you saved my life or some crap[1]. Personally I don't recall anything like that, but you know what old men are like, right? So when he heard you were in trouble and out of your depth, he ordered me to come and bail you out. He said, 'Don't you move from his side till he's in the clear, d'you hear!" She did a creditable imitation of her father's cut-glass English accent, and then added in broad Texan, "So I am just doing ma' job, y'all. We done?"

"I guess so. But I don't like it."

She winked. "That's 'cause you're a big, macho bull of a man and you don't like skinny little girls saving your ass. C'mon. Let's get moving and make a plan." She started walking back toward the house, talking over her shoulder as she went. "We should aim to be in Spain by tomorrow morning."

I stopped for a moment, forcing her to stop and turn to look at me. I was visualizing the map of France, with Spain stuck on the end and the Pyrenees cutting them off from each other, but was momentarily distracted by how attractive she was, as a person. I frowned and coughed to clear my throat.

"We head for Bilbao. That's about five hundred and forty miles, via Bordeaux, Henday, Irun. We take it easy because we don't want to be stopped. Five hundred and forty divided by fifty miles an hour…"

I paused to think and she said, "Just short of eleven. Ten point eight."

I looked at my watch. It was just before two o'clock. "That gets us there at midnight. Twenty-four hours short of Armageddon."

"We can't think about that anymore. We have one focus." She lifted her index finger. "And one focus only: Colonel James Gordon."

I went and stood close to her. "Why are you doing this, Gallin? Seriously. You don't need to."

She punched me gently on the chest. "Coz I love you, pal. Oh, and," she laughed, "Bordeaux wines followed by Basque meat, are you kidding me?" She turned away again and headed for the car. "Now stop being a big girl's blouse and get your ass in gear."

I heard myself give a troubled sigh and followed after her. I am not big on feelings, but right then I felt grateful to Gabriel Gallin, her father, and grateful for Aila Gallin.

———

WE TOOK the driving in shifts. She did the first four hours as far as Poitiers. There we took a break at the Intermarché gas station and had some cake and coffee at the Roof Café. Over coffee I told Gallin:

"Just a few miles south of here, Gallin, was one of the most important battles in military history."

She raised an eyebrow at me. "No kidding."

"The battle of Poitiers."

She bit into a large slice of carrot cake. "Really?"

"Really. 19th September, 1356. King Edward III of England had crossed the Channel and was raiding deep into northern France. His two sons, meanwhile, were plundering Normandy and central France.

"King Jean II of France, hearing that the English were plundering basically all of his kingdom, crossed the River Loire to challenge them. Edward headed south as quickly as his laden baggage train would allow, and the French intercepted him three miles east of Poitiers, where we are right now.

"Edward, who was a very smart tactician, chose his position well in what would become a master class on how to defeat overwhelmingly superior numbers, and a blueprint to be followed many times in the future by the British in their wars with the French, Napoleon—and the rest of the world as they built their empire.

"He positioned his men at the top of a slope, protected on the left by a marsh and a stream. Ahead of him he had a hedge protecting him from the field, and on his right flank, where he was exposed, he placed his wagons. This was good planning, but his stroke of military genius was to line up his archers behind the hedge and keep a small reserve force of cavalry on his right flank.

"In the early morning of 19th September, the French began their attack. They had a force of some forty thousand men, compared to the twelve thousand Englishmen. Their first move was a rather unimaginative charge with the cavalry, attempting to storm through the only gap in the hedge, which was just wide enough for about four men riding abreast. Naturally, as they reached the gap, the English archers showered them with arrows. As they fell, dead and dying men and horses blocked the gap. Most of the knights were pinned under their fallen mounts, and those who weren't were finished off with swords and knives.

"The second attack, led by the Dauphin himself, marched up the slope on foot. They were again showered with arrows. Imagine what it must have been like, Gallin: three thousand arrows per second raining down, the sky darkened by clouds of whistling, screaming barbs shot from bows with draw weights of anything up to a hundred and eighty pounds draw weight.

"The soldiers eventually reached the hedge, having suffered heavy losses on their march through hell, and engaged the English in heavy fighting, but Edward brought up his reserves and they were repulsed.

"In what should have been the third French attack, the soldiers, led by the young Duc d'Orléans, were so overcome with fear at what they had seen so far that they fled the battlefield in disarray. So, finally, the French king himself led the final advance toward the English.

"Edward once again showed his genius and responded by ordering his small reserve cavalry force to gallop around the French flank and attack from the rear, while his entire army charged the French from the front. The fighting was intense, with many English archers fighting with knives and hand axes because their supply of arrows was exhausted. Eventually the French army, devastated by the archers in the first attacks, was overwhelmed, along with the king and his bodyguard. King Jean was taken into captivity and held until a vast ransom was paid in 1360. Many of his leading nobles lost their lives that day, and many more were taken captive and ransomed, like the king.

"Of the twelve thousand Englishmen at the battle, one thousand died. Of the forty thousand French, two thousand five hundred died and another two thousand six hundred were taken captive. The remaining thirty-four thousand nine hundred Frenchmen fled. It is interesting to note, Gallin, that the French soldiers who fled, outnumbered the English three to one."

She sat a while, sipping her coffee and regarding me with narrowed eyes.

"You know I am English, right? We studied Poitiers at school. It was like a rerun of Crecy ten years earlier. Only at Crecy, by the end of the battle King Philip's brother, Charles II of Alençon, King John of Bohemia and Louis II of Nevers, the Count of Flanders and one thousand five hundred knights and squires were dead, and Edward went on to besiege and take Calais. The French lost fourteen thousand men out of thirty-five thousand—including the cream of the aristocracy—and the English had lost two hundred of their sixteen thousand troops. What was your point?"

I shrugged. "I just thought as we were here I would impress you with my knowledge of history. I was also thinking about underdogs triumphing against over-whelming odds."

She nodded. "I hear you." She watched me a moment, then asked, "So what was the stroke of genius that the Black Prince displayed that would become a blueprint for battles to come?"

I smiled. "That power must be projected. The French considered the bow a knightly or kingly weapon appropriate for hunting. But the English put it in the hands of yeomen and turned it into the most fearsome military tool of the age, because it projected lethal power deep into the enemy ranks long before the enemy was within striking distance."

"That is what the Russians want to do to us with this satellite."

"Yup." I nodded. "Whether he knows it or not, Putin is applying the lessons Edward III taught his son at Crecy. Project your power to the perimeter."

She set down her empty cup. "So how do we go about doing that, Mason? How do we project our power to the perimeter, and bring down an overwhelmingly powerful enemy?"

"I don't know." I looked out through the plate-glass Euro-window at the anonymous Euro-gas station, which might have been any gas station anywhere in the Western world, and thought about power and violence. "I don't know," I said again. "One of us is going to have to channel Edward III."

I took the car then, down the N10 to Angouleme, and from there, as dusk quickened into evening, to Bordeaux. We bypassed the city, crossing the Garonne River over the Aquitaine Bridge, seeing little more than what looked like a giant Christmas tree on our left. After that it was right at Bois de Cotor onto the A63 all the way through the dark, nocturnal fields, to Hendaye. The last French town before Spain.

Before COVID you used to be able to cross back and forth from France to Spain via the Pont International over the River Bidasoa. After COVID the border was closed till 2021, when it opened cautiously. Now they make random checks, not to see if you're carrying bombs or drugs, but to see if you have your digital vaccine passport.

We had phoned ahead and booked a room at the Hotel Chambres de d'Hôtes Hor Dago, and there we dropped the car in the hotel parking lot, hit the room and collapsed into bed for a good night's sleep. In the morning we had a hearty breakfast and went out to make like tourists, strolling arm-in-arm through the cute, medieval town. At the International Bridge we strolled across with Gallin hanging on my elbow, stopping to look down at the sparkling water, ignoring the police clustered outside their vans. They were on the lookout for anyone who didn't have that hive glaze to their eyes.

After a short while Gallin squeezed my arm and looked up at me like I was the man of her dreams and said, "We're in Spain. We need to rent a car."

I gave her an affectionate hug. "You say the sweetest things. I booked a car online last night, while you were sleeping. We just need to take a cab to the airport."

"See?" she said. "That's why I married you."

EIGHT

IRUN HAS A CUTE MEDIEVAL AIRPORT, WITH NICE terraced houses with red gabled roofs just a hundred yards from the runway. True to the Spanish genius for making things hard to understand, the airport is physically located inside the town of Irun, on the banks of the river Bidasoa, which separates Hendaye from Irun, but it is in fact San Sebastian Airport—San Sebastian which is thirteen miles farther down the coast, and a completely different city. In fact, just in case that was too easy to grasp, the town where San Sebastian Airport is located is not even Irun—though everybody calls it Irun, it is actually Hondarribia, and is, like the airport, physically inside Irun. But, as nobody has ever heard of Hondarribia, they call it Irun.

So, when I told the taxi driver to take us to Irun airport he shook his head and said, "No Irun airport. No airport in Irun."

"I can see it," I said, pointing. "It's over there. Look, there is an aeroplane landing right now."

"No Irun airport. San Sebastian airport."

"So, San Sebastian Airport is in Irun?"

"No in Irun. In Hondarribia. You wanna go or you no wanna go?"

Gallin explained it to me in the back of the cab as we pulled away

"It's like Boulder, Colorado, wants to build an airport, but they're nervous because the Rockies are too close and they fear the planes might crash. So they build their airport in Wiggins, which is nice and flat, but still call it Boulder Airport. But they're not Spanish."

"Who?"

"You said the Spanish had a genius for making things hard to understand. But these people are not Spanish. They're Basque. They are different in every way. Temperament, culture, architecture, even genetically. Genetically the Basques are closer to the English than to anybody else."

"That would explain it. Two London Airports, neither of which is in London, one is in Gatwick and the other in Heathrow, and the one that *is* in London is called City Airport."

"Shut up, Mason." Her phone was ringing and she pulled it from her jacket.

We pulled up and while she walked away along the shaded front of the airport I paid the driver. He went away and Gallin walked back, putting her phone away. Over the Atlantic behind her, big ugly clouds were piling up.

"The office. We get the results on the DNA and the prints. Captain Joseph Fyodorovich, Russian special forces. No great surprise at this stage. Also, Gordon's not in Madrid."

"Where is he? Do they know?"

"Yeah, he's in Andorra."

"What the hell is he doing in Andorra?"

"As it turns out, that is actually a good question. Let's get the car and get going. We have to go to Bilbao first."

She stepped through the sliding doors and we headed for the car rental stands. The pretty girl with the jet-black ponytail wanted to give us a Mercedes. Gallin said she refused to drive a German car and after half an hour they gave us a Range Rover.

As we pulled out of the airport along the N638, the perfect blue skies had turned to heavy, gunmetal gray and it had started to rain. I sat in silence watching the lush, green rolling hills and the dense forests of oak, ash, hazels and fir bowing and tossing in the downpour. Gallin was right, this was not what you thought of as Spanish. Even the houses and villages we passed, many of them half-timbered and gable-roofed, did not look Spanish.

We joined the freeway at the Alcampo shopping mall, inserting ourselves among the spray and hiss of the traffic. Gallin started to talk, staring hard ahead through the rain.

"We are going to Bilbao to meet a contact. He's a British agent."

That made me look at her. "SIS? He could be with the Five Eyes and he could be cooperating with the CIA."

"The Institute have vetted him. He has cooperated with us for a long time. MI6 is as worried about the Rusenko issue as you are. Don't forget, London gets taken out along with all the US cities. He is keen to help, with the blessings of London."

I grunted. "OK."

"He will brief us on Colonel James Gordon and his trip to Andorra. He will also provide us with papers to get us into Andorra."

I frowned at her. "How does he have my photograph?"

"We have you on file, darling. Just as you have me on file."

I looked at my watch. It was half past ten. Three thirty AM in New York. I wondered if they'd arrived yet, and whether Nero had been able to swing it with Groom Lake. It was impossible not to wonder how long we had left. Gallin glanced at me and seemed to read my thoughts.

"There's nothing we can do about that. It's not in our hands anymore. You may as well wonder whether you're going to get hit by a car in the next ten minutes. All we can do is clear your name and expose the mole."

It was little more than an hour's drive through rain-washed landscapes that were green and lush and had nothing whatever to do with arid sierras and bullfights. To me Spain was Arizona and southern California without the technology or the rednecks. This was something else.

We entered Bilbao from the north, into the old town. It was a city of massive, solid eighteenth and nineteenth-century buildings, no higher than five stories, that were steeped in gravitas and dignity, the way old cities used to be. The streetlamps were all Victorian cast iron, and made you want to reach for your bowler hat and your umbrella.

We made our way through narrow streets full of shops and tobacconists, all with warm, homely façades that spoke of neighborhoods where everybody knew each other. Neither of us had spoken much for a while, but Gallin said suddenly, into the silence: "It's human."

I watched her face for a long moment as she navigated the streets, then nodded. It was human.

"It's weird," she added suddenly.

"What is?"

"How that same instinct to create a safe place for you and your family, a place you can recognize and call home, can become so twisted that it ends up ready to annihilate a hundred million people over eight cities." She glanced at me. "It starts with, 'This is our safe area, for me and my tribe.' Then becomes, 'To be truly safe I need that bit of land there too. And I need weapons to protect it, and walls.' After which it becomes, 'My tribe and my land are better than yours, you are an existential threat to my tribe and you aren't even really human anyway. So it's OK if I just march in and wipe you out.'"

We turned in off a small circus with gardens and a fountain in the center, and pulled up outside a large café-restaurant-cake shop affair that would have looked right at home in Paris. There were chairs outside, under an awning. The rain had eased, but the plane trees were glimmering with fresh rain, and the smell of coffee and cakes from inside was rich on the air. It reminded my stomach we hadn't eaten since our early breakfast.

We hunched into our shoulders and moved past the chairs and the parasols to a tall, wooden door set into the gray, granite face of one of those massive eighteenth-century buildings. There were twelve buttons set into a plate in the wall, with a microphone and a minute camera lens. Gallin pressed one of the buttons and we waited, staring at each other in a way that should have been embarrassing but wasn't.

"Si?"

"Mr. Marshal?"

"Speaking."

"I wonder if you've heard from the hospital?"

"Not in the last three weeks."

"What steps have you taken?"

"The necessary ones. Come on up. Top floor."

The door buzzed and she pushed it open.

The entrance hall was narrow with high ceilings, a checkerboard floor and a spiral mahogany staircase. We took the elevator to the sixth floor and when we stepped out onto the landing there was a door open at the end of the hall with a slim man silhouetted in it. As we approached I saw he was in his late thirties, he had floppy blond hair and a silk cravat under a blue shirt.

"Aila, so nice to see you. Come on in." As I approached he held out his hand. "I'm Kit, no need for your name if you prefer, but I may as well tell you I know who you are." We shook. "Come on in. I think everyone in the Western world is reading your file at the moment. You're on the news. Did you know?"

"On the news?"

He closed the door and pointed to the living room. Gallin went in and I followed her. It was comfortably modern, a bachelor's flat with ashtrays, a well-stocked bar and used coffee cups left for later. Two sets of windows overlooked the street outside. He had a news channel on the TV. Gallin sat on the sofa and I leaned against the wall. They had an English reporter reporting from Paris. He was talking to the camera from the Quai de la Corse, overlooking the river at the top of the steps where Mira Finn's body had been found.

"Details are still very sketchy, Martin, and we may never know the full story. Interestingly, though, even regular sources within the diplomatic and intelligence communities are refusing to speak. But what I have been able to gather so far is that an American, one Alexander Mason, resident in Washington, DC, is being sought by American law enforcement *and* the Central Intelligence Agency, presumably in connection with the murder and torture of Mira Finn, an Irish subject who, allegedly, worked with American intelligence."

They cut back to the studio, where the anchorman was frowning.

"David, you say that both American law enforcement *and* the CIA are searching for this man, but what about the French authorities?"

"Bizarrely, Martin, the French authorities are remaining utterly silent on the matter. Some sources, whom I cannot name, are saying that Mason is an American agent who has gone rogue, and that the French are taking the frankly unprecedented step of standing aside and allowing American agents to operate freely on French soil."

"And is this man considered a public threat, David?"

"The CIA are saying that he is highly trained and very dangerous, and should under no circumstances be approached. So far everything seems to point to some kind of operation within the intelligence community that has gone badly wrong. However, if he *is* on the run and *is* versed in field craft, then it is conceivable that he could become dangerous if cornered. Police are advising the public that if they see this man," my photograph was displayed on the screen, looking suitably grainy and psychotic, "that they should not approach him but contact the local police, or call this number."

A number was displayed on the screen and Kit switched off the TV. He sat in an armchair facing us and rubbed his hands over his knees.

"Right, I have for you, courtesy of the Mossad, two passports, driver's licenses, two credit cards which, I am told by Mordecai, hack automatically into Mark Zuckerberg's private accounts in Panama. So knock yourselves out with those. And in view of the media attention you have been attracting since last night, Alex, you are Bruce Harrington. I have taken the liberty of having a chap I know do a bit of Photoshop magic on your picture, and I would strongly suggest you apply some specs and a moustache. I can supply both if you want them. Aila, you are Jo, Joanna."

I interrupted. "That's great. Thanks. Listen, before we go any further. Do you mind telling me why the SIS is helping me?"

He frowned and then smiled and then raised an eyebrow at me.

"A number of reasons, Alex. In the first place we would rather not have London erased from the map by a nuclear strike if it can be avoided, and from what Aila is telling us, that is precisely what Putin plans to do. In the second place we would rather not have our closest allies erased from the map either. Thirdly, even if you have chaps working on preventing that strike, it seems very important to us to find out who has infiltrated the president of the USA's most intimate inner circle of advisers. Especially," his frown deepened, "as it seems that it might actually be the president himself."

I scowled at him. "What the hell gave you that idea?"

He smiled. "We do have some experience in analyzing intelligence, Alex. There were four people who could have leaked Mira's role in extracting Rusenko. You and Nero, General O'Connor and the president himself. Nero is off the hook because it would make no sense for him to set up the whole operation and then alert the Russians of what he had done, at the last moment. Let's face it, Nero would have done a much better job of the whole thing, and he would have been in a position to have ensured it worked." He sighed apologetically and added, "Also, and at risk of laboring a point, if it had been Nero, they would have caught you by now.

"Almost the same argument applies to you. You were briefed on practically every detail of the operation. You would have been in a position to ensure that Rusenko was caught along with his French contacts. Instead, you got saddled as the scapegoat, if you'll forgive the mixed metaphors." He spread his hands and gave a little laugh. "Exactly the opposite is true of the other two candidates. Neither of them was directly involved in setting up the operation. Both of them were therefore potentially able to cock it up and let Rusenko get away. Nevertheless, both excluded from suspicion because of *who* they were, not because they couldn't have done it.

"Now, according to our files, General O'Connor is known for his longstanding hostility to Moscow and the Kremlin, he has initiated a number of backroom campaigns to have Russian oligarchs stripped of their assets on the grounds of money laundering, and during the Russian invasion of Ukraine he was vocal on the subject of sending troops to assist the Ukrainians.

"It seems to me highly unlikely that this man would then betray his country to assist Putin in either attacking the USA or holding it hostage."

Gallin said, "Hold on. Mason didn't know about the satellites, or what Rusenko was going to the States for. It's possible the general didn't either."

"In the first place, as a military general acting as military adviser to the president, that is so unlikely as to be almost impossible. In the second place, even if it were true, it is hard to imagine General Patrick O'Connor, one of the most anti-Russian generals on the staff, betraying his country to the Russians. On the other hand..."

He paused and looked at me apologetically. "Forgive me if you are fond of this president, but he has a long track record, going right back to his early college years, of Russian sympathy. Everything from volunteering at the Museum of Russian Icons at Harvard and joining the American Socialist Party, to corresponding with Mikhail Gorbachev and Gennady Yanayev to discuss what they thought went wrong with the socialist project in Russia. He is still a proponent of several ideas he is trying to put through Congress which amount to huge hikes in tax-and-spend, and increasing the powers of the federal government over the state legislatures. Strip away the titles and look at the CV—what you call résumé—of each man, and the main suspect leaps out at you."

I shook my head. "It's inconceivable. I can't buy it."

He laughed. "Well, I'm afraid that doesn't tell us

anything about the president. It just tells us about your ability to conceive. But in the end, the bottom line is, you don't need to buy it. You just need to follow the evidence and allow the evidence to speak. If I am wrong, no one will be happier than me. But if I am right, for God's sake don't cover it up. Blow the lid off it and expose whatever it is that has gone wrong with the system."

I felt suddenly very tired and lowered myself into a chair. "OK," I said, "I'll bear an open mind. Meantime, you had better tell us about Colonel James Gordon, and why he is in Andorra."

NINE

Some hours earlier, at eleven-fifty PM local time, a Gulfstream G650 had come in low over the Dixie National Forest in Utah. It had skimmed the hills to the south of the small town of Caliente and flown just a couple of hundred feet above the Jumbled Hills that encircle Area 51 to the east. Then it banked right and approached to land at Homey Airport, on the edge of the salt flats that are Groom Lake.

It touched down with a squeal of tortured rubber and the high whine of the turbines, and taxied to a halt on the tarmac, facing the glaring headlamps of two Land Rovers and a Hummer. The brilliant halo distorted the shapes of eight men into hazy silhouettes. Three were Marines, a fourth was their gunnery sergeant. The other three included the man known only as Nero, who stood six foot four and weighed four hundred and fifty pounds; beside him, legs akimbo and stiff as a ramrod, was Brigadier General Bill

Clancy, overall commander of the Groom Lake facility, and behind him his driver and bodyguard.

The plane came to a halt with a dying whine and, as the cabin door opened and the steps lowered to the tarmac, the Marine sergeant ran forward with his men to escort the two passengers down the steps. Nero observed them with care, taking in every detail. They both looked willowy, old and tired. The desert air was cold and he saw them shudder. He advanced on them with his hand outstretched.

"Dr. Patel, Dr. Rusenko. This is Brigadier General Clancy. We have little or no time. Please come with me. As you know, every minute counts."

He said all this as the four men shook hands and he ushered them toward the Land Rovers. The pilot of the jet was instructed to refuel immediately and leave American airspace. The doctors were ushered into a Land Rover with Nero and a Marine driver and, with the Hummer in the vanguard and the brigadier general at the rear. they drove at speed along an asphalt road that led behind a giant hangar and up into the hills, toward a complex of smaller buildings. One of these was a large hangar-like structure with a dome in the center of the roof, like an observatory. The main entrance was open and the two Land Rovers roared in and squealed to a halt, setting up wild echoes under the high ceiling. The Hummer drew across the entrance. The Marines leapt down and spread across the entryway, with their assault rifles at the ready.

Nero, the general and the two scientists climbed down from their truck as a redheaded man in a white lab coat hurried toward them from the bowels of the hangar, where a spiral, steel staircase climbed toward an upper floor. Beyond it Nero observed, ranged against the walls and apparently at random around the vast floor area, machines and computer terminals whose function he could only guess at, this being, as it was, the laser lab.

The general advanced toward the hurrying figure.

"Dr. Hemmings, allow me to introduce…"

Hemmings interrupted him. "Rusenko, I am delighted to see you in one piece, and Dr. Patel, I am so glad you have come as well." He glanced at the brigadier general, muttered, "Yes, thank you, General," and gestured toward the staircase, addressing the doctors again. "Shall we? I'll explain what we have at our disposal as we go. Do you in fact *have* the coordinates? We also need to know: is the satellite completely invisible, or *almost* invisible?"

The five men made their way across the floor, the three scientists apparently unaware of the men who followed them. Rusenko was saying, "It is *almost* undetectable, but not completely. I am assuming they have not changed coordinates since Paris—not much, anyhow. It is anyone's guess, but they have very limited scope. Changing the coordinates will affect their ability to target all the cities at same time. The coordinates I set were perfect location. On the other hand, maintaining the location puts target at risk."

The general growled. "But our window of opportunity is so small, gentlemen, they may have chosen to take that risk."

Rusenko nodded. "It is possible. In any case, I have spent the last couple of days working out the best alternative coordinates for the attack. We need to check them all systematically. We may find a trace of heat, a trace of echo…"

His final words were drowned out by the squealing

brakes of several vehicles arriving on the asphalt outside. Seconds later there was the slamming of doors and the fearsome bellow of a marine gunnery sergeant's voice.

"*Halt! You may not enter! This is a restricted area!*"

They all stopped and turned. Nero saw on the forecourt of the hangar a Jeep and a truck. From the Jeep had descended General Patrick O'Connor, large and red-faced, a captain and two grunts. From the truck had jumped down somewhere in the region of twenty armed men. He turned to the three scientists and hissed, "*Move! Go! Go now!*" To General Clancy he snapped, "With me! Make a noise!"

From the entrance he could hear O'Connor shouting. "Do you know who I am, sar'nt? I am assuming control of this operation on the direct orders of the president! *Stand down!*"

"*Sir, no sir!*"

Nero, with a voice the size of a Megatron, descended on the intruders. "*Nobody is assuming control of anything here, General O'Connor! The supreme commander of this base is Brigadier General William Clancy, and he shall remain in command until he receives orders relieving him of his command! Have you any such orders?*"

The general's eyes narrowed and his freckled face flushed.

"Nero! I might have guessed I'd find you here!"

"You will find me in many more places in the near future, General, you may be sure of that!"

"Tell these men to stand down! I have orders direct from the president..."

Nero cut him short with a voice that would have busted windows at the Vienna Opera House.

"You! You claim you have orders! And well you might! But I have no orders from the president, and neither has the supreme commander of this base! Where you, sir, have no jurisdiction!" He turned to the brigadier general, who seemed content to leave the bellowing to Nero. "Have you any orders from the president, Brigadier General, relieving you of your command?"

When he answered he spoke quietly, with supreme authority. "No sir."

General O'Connor, with a smile that could only be described as smug, reached inside his jacket pocket and withdrew an envelope bearing the White House crest. He handed it to the gunnery sergeant.

"Here y'are, son. Hand this over to your ex-commanding officer."

The gunnery sergeant saluted smartly, took the envelope and handed it over to the brigadier general, who took it and opened it. He scanned it a moment, then looked at General O'Connor.

"This is a letter, signed by the president, instructing me to hand over control of the base to you, General O'Connor, and to place this man under arrest." He gestured at Nero. "Along with Dr. Rusenko and Dr. Patel."

He held the letter up for General O'Connor to see and carefully folded it and tore it in half, after which he tore it in half again.

O'Connor's face turned puce. He turned to his men and yelled, *"Men, prepare to open fire!"*

Brigadier General Bill Clancy stepped forward, edged between his men and stood beside his gunnery sergeant. Again he spoke with quiet authority.

"Pat, before you do anything real stupid, like murdering a brigadier general and four Marines, as well as the head of the Office of the Director of the Intelligence Network, maybe you had better inform yourself, and the president, of exactly how this works." He looked past the general and addressed the captain who stood behind him. "This goes for you and your men too, Captain. You would be complicit in murder, and possibly also in treason."

O'Connor snarled, "You hand over Rusenko right now, Clancy, or I swear I will storm this hangar!"

The brigadier general didn't blink. He continued to speak quietly.

"It has long been established, Pat, that this base does not come under the direct control of the president. He is not the first to attempt to take control of what goes on here, and believe me, far more powerful men than he have tried and failed. We are charged here with preserving national security, and that is exactly what we are going to do. Right now, Pat, there is an expert Marine marksman with a bead on your temple. In addition, there are two hundred US Marines surrounding you and your men. On my order my expert marksman will take you out, and then the Marines will move in. And you will go down in history as the general who betrayed his country and assisted the Russians in attempting a nuclear strike against the USA."

Again he looked past the general at the men behind him.

"You boys want to be on that roster?" They were very quiet for a moment, and then, one by one, began to lower their arms. Brigadier General Clancy said, "Captain, place this man under close arrest. General, hand over your weapon to the captain. You are hereby relieved of your command."

Nobody moved. The two generals stared at each other while their men remained paralyzed. Finally O'Connor spoke.

"All right, Clancy, I'm going and I'm taking my men with me. But we'll be back. You can bet your ass on that. And when I return you'll be facing a court martial on charges of treason."

The brigadier general nodded. "When the truth comes out, Pat, we'll see who faces what charges." The brigadier general turned to his gunnery sergeant. "Gunny, escort the general off the base. And Pat," he turned back to the general, "in case you get any crazy ideas, you will be watched every inch of the way to Crystal Springs, and if we need to we can deploy the most advanced weaponry on the planet at a moment's notice."

General Pat O'Connor grunted and marched back to his trucks. They wheeled and in a few seconds were rumbling away toward the exit road.

Nero was already hurrying toward the spiral staircase. He climbed the steps with surprising agility for a man his size. At the top he found what looked very much like a traditional telescope, but where telescopes of the sort at Mount Palomar have a vertical opening to allow the telescope access to the sky, this dome had a kind of leaf shutter that retracted to open the entire dome. And the "telescope," instead of ending in a large lens, had a large, silver ball which seemed to move independently, and had a number of protrusions extending from it.

He found Dr. Hemmings, Dr. Patel and Dr. Rusenko gathered around a bank of four computer monitors, muttering to each other and pointing at one particular screen which was dark and divided into quadrants. As Nero approached he observed that as well as being divided into quadrants, it also displayed a map of the stars.

"It's taken care of. Nobody should bother us now for a good twenty-four hours."

"Good, good," Rusenko muttered, eyeing the screen. "More time than we need."

Hemmings sighed and turned to Nero. "It is still primitive."

"The laser?"

"The laser. The power source is bulky and heavy, but the business end is pretty quick. We aim to get it down to the size of a rifle, but the problem is the energy supply. Anything less than a small reactor and your beam starts fanning and dissipating."

Rusenko nodded. "We have same problem. Fusion reactor is solution, but until we can control magnetic containment fields, nothing to do."

"Gentlemen," Nero boomed in an outburst of irritation, "have we found the satellite?"

"We are looking, but I tell you it has stealth capability. It absorbs light. This area here it must be, but...," he spread his hands and nodded slowly, "this area here is like five hundred miles of empty space. We make random shots and maybe in four years we burn somebody's ass on Proxima B."

All three of them laughed like he had said something hilarious.

"Gentlemen, time is of the essence. Have we a strategy other than merely staring at a computer monitor?"

Rusenko looked up and stared at the wall. He spread his

hands, stood and walked in a large circle, saying, "So...
So... So..."

Nero barked, "Dr. Rusenko, we have not the time for
theatrics!"

"How can I explain? Great Architect! Give me words to
explain! This is not Vietnam in sixties, it is not Dresden in
forties. We cannot carpet bomb space. This is beam, less than
one inch in diameter. When we aim, we are aiming at target
less than one inch in diameter! Is logical, or I am crazy? We
deviate *one millimeter* down here, and in orbit this signifies
many miles deviation! We *must* find where is he, the satellite,
before we make commitment to shoot. When we shoot, we
declare ourself."

Dr. Hemmings interrupted Rusenko, "OK, Nero, sir,
here is the problem. We have the sector based on Dr.
Rusenko's coordinates. If Putin is aiming to strike at New
York, Washington, San Francisco and LA, and, we assume,
almost simultaneously London, Brussels, Berlin and Paris,
then he *must* be in this sector of the sky, directly above
Bermuda. But as Dr. Rusenko has pointed out, we have to
be minutely precise, because a millimeter's deviation at this
end, can signify being several miles off target in that sector."

The stairs clattered behind them and the brigadier
general appeared. He looked drawn and tired.

"The base is secured. General O'Connor is under lock
and key and guarded by four Marines. It would take a full-on
military operation to get in here, and we probably have the
technology to repulse it. Now we just need your man to
come through, and for the satellite to show up. How are we
doing?"

Rusenko shook his head and sighed. It was a ragged

sound. "It is invisible. It deflects radar and absorbs cold laser and sunlight. It does not reflect. We are searching, searching for some small giveaway trace. But he is invisible."

"How long have we got?"

Nero said, "We don't know exactly, but the clock is running down. The attack could be triggered at any moment in the next twelve hours."

"So what's the plan? How do we find it?"

There was a deathly silence until Rusenko said, "No plan. Just we look."

The brigadier general shook his head. "No. I am sorry, but I am in the presence of the finest minds in the world, we are facing nuclear devastation in the USA and Europe, and nobody can come up with anything better than, 'We just have to keep looking for it'?"

Rusenko turned on the brigadier, throwing his hands in the air. "However intelligent or stupid I am, the reality is the same! I cannot change reality just because I am clever! If the satellite is invisible it is invisible! If I have IQ of one-seventy, can I see air? No! Why? Because it is invisible! If I have IQ of one-eighty, can I see electrons? No. Why? Because they are invisible! We have collective IQ of nearly one thousand. Can we see satellite? No. Why? *Because it is invisible!*"

Nero said, quietly, "But with an IQ one-seventy, you could find a way to make the invisible visible."

Rusenko gazed at him resentfully. "So, how can you make my satellite visible. You are going to pour talcum powder on it?"

"No, we haven't the time for that."

"So what then?"

"We have two options. I am sure you will correct me if I

am wrong. But if the satellite is forced to move it will have to fire up thrusters, which will create a heat signature in that area. Perhaps so small we would not see it, unless we were looking for it. Am I right?"

He nodded and shrugged. "Yes, but how do we make it move?"

"Well, that is the clever bit, Rusenko. We have been focusing too hard on how *we* might see *it*. What we need to be thinking about is how to make *it* see *us*."

The three scientists, with a collective IQ of five hundred, frowned at him.

TEN

He had disappeared down a long corridor, and when he returned it was to tell us that Rosalia was making us some roast beef sandwiches, and would bring us some cold beers. Then he sat back in his comfortable, worn armchair and crossed one elegant leg over the other. Outside the sun had poked through the Atlantic clouds and I could hear the faint chatter of starlings in the plane trees, the sigh of tires on wet asphalt and desultory honk of cars.

"There are colonels and colonels," he said at last. "Some colonels command bases and lead their men into combat. They are men of action, sort of glorified sergeant majors, and they like it that way." He paused and gazed out the window. "Others, usually men involved to a greater or lesser extent in the intelligence community, rise to occupy offices and places of eminence that some generals would envy. They become presidential advisors and have their own offices in the Pentagon. These are quiet, trusted men you do not often see in photographs, who carry a lot more weight politically than you would expect from a lowly colonel."

I said, "And James Gordon is one such colonel?"

"Oh yes," he accompanied the affirmation with a soft laugh. "Colonel James Gordon has forged a career for himself by not being noticed by anybody except the right people—the people he wants to be noticed by. And among those people were General Pat O'Connor, who became something of a mentor for the colonel, and the then future president. Both the general and the colonel have been instrumental, in their way, in getting this president into office."

"A little surprising," it was Gallin. "O'Connor is your classic Republican hawk. If he is Gordon's mentor, I am guessing Gordon follows the same line, so what are they doing supporting a president who is on the dripping side of wet?"

"That is a good question, and it's a question the intelligence community has been asking itself for a long time. The simple answer is that so far nobody knows. But it may be that we have just found out."

I asked, "What do you mean?"

"It sounds like the more extravagant kind of conspiracy theory, but this may have been a very long game plan. We know that back in the days of the Cold War the Soviets used to plant sleepers who might well go their entire lives without ever being activated. We know that Putin was and is a loyal Soviet, whose deepest wish is to return Russia to its former glory. So this begs the question, were O'Connor and Gordon sleepers, planted for the purpose of getting close to the president? Of course, back when they were planted, they had no idea who the president would be.

"On the other hand, we also have to ask..."

He paused and Gallin supplied the missing words, "Was the president?"

He shrugged and made a "Why not?" face. The living room door opened and a plump woman with pink, smiling cheeks came in bearing an improbably large tray with a vast stack of very thick beef, lettuce and tomato sandwiches, and three large jugs of beer. She set the tray down on the dining table at the far end of the room and distributed the goods with a smile that said she was proud of her work. We thanked her and she left.

I took a generous bite out of the sandwich and followed it with a generous pull on the beer. When I had done justice to this Basque woman's talents I said, "I don't buy that the president is a sleeper. I can't. It's going too far."

"And I'm not saying he is," he replied, chewing around his words. "What I am saying is that there is something in the President-O'Connor-Gordon setup that reeks of sleepers and is hard to explain any other way."

Gallin wiped her mouth with the back of her hand and added, "Camp geni dat." I caught her eye and smiled. She took a pull of beer and repeated, "Can't deny that."

I nodded. "But the most we can conclude is that they have an odd relationship which politically is not readily explainable. Anything more is speculation."

"Correct," it was Marshal. "Though I think you can go one step further and say that the president apparently keeps very bad company and very bad advisers."

"OK, so what about Andorra?"

Outside there was a distant roll of thunder, the sky went

suddenly dark and after a moment large raindrops began to spatter the windowpanes.

"As I am sure you know, aside from having a very sweet tax setup, Andorra is often used by billionaires, and people of political power and influence, as a place to get together out of the public eye and chat about where to trigger wars and economic crises so as best to benefit their own particular business interests."

I arched an eyebrow at him. "Next you'll be telling me Andorra was founded by the Illuminati."

He smiled. "No, but I will tell you that the Bilderberg Group met there a couple of years ago at the Grand Continental, and one of the topics on the agenda was world population."

"You're kidding me."

"Actually, I never joke about these topics, Mason. If you don't believe me you are welcome to look it up on Google. The Bilderberg Group has a website. You may remember it was something of a fracas, a bomb exploded, a fire broke out and several of the more eminent attendees were killed. It was quite a sensation."[1]

"OK, so what are you telling me, that Colonel James Gordon is a member of the Bilderberg Group, and he has gone to Andorra to meet with Adam Weishaupt and declare *Ewige Blumenkraft*?"

"A little facetious, Mr. Mason."

"Can you blame me?"

He smiled pleasantly and asked me, "Perhaps you would like to explain to me why Colonel Gordon is in Andorra?"

"OK, *touché*. I'll shut up and let you tell me."

Gallin smiled and winked at me. "Good plan, big guy."

"As you can imagine, we are as worried as you are about the situation with Putin and Rusenko. So we've had our people in Madrid keeping tabs on Colonel Gordon. When we found he was going to Andorra for no apparent reason, we decided to cast around and see who else was headed that way."

Gallin asked, "And?"

"There are a handful of luxury hotels, and one or two that have the kind of security arrangements you'd want for, for example, a Bilderberg gathering. So we started by checking their bookings." He saw me frown and smiled. "Aside from having people working there, we have some pretty clever hackers on our staff too."

"So who is coming to meet him?"

"General O'Connor is a major consultant for AAA—Anglo-American Armaments—a firm that deals internationally in weapons. Originally, as the name suggests, it dealt mainly with American and British manufacturers, but then started expanding into wider markets. Two years ago fifty-one percent of its shares were bought by a consortium of Russian and Hong Kong billionaires. Principal members of the board were replaced, including the CEO. The CEO now is Boris Semenov, one of those Russian oligarchs we keep hearing about. He was stripped of practically all his Western assets after the invasion of Ukraine, but he has enough investments in Russia and the Far East for it really not to affect him. And needless to say, AAA Inc. had the foresight to shift its main office from London to Hong Kong before the invasion."

"And he is visiting Andorra."

"Correct. He is booked in at the Grand Continental, as is Peter Romano."

"Who the hell is Peter Romano?"

Marshal laughed softly. "I didn't know until we looked into it. He is the ultimate Man in Gray. He owns a publicity and social media company in DC, called simply Cognition. That is to say, he owns sixty percent of the stock, but he is the sleeping partner, leaving the day-to-day administration and running of the company to his partner, Abraham Gold, and a team of Ivy League psychologists.

"He, meantime, is a consultant to a small group of hand-picked corporate giants in the field of IT and social media—and, the jewel in his crown, Andy Costello. Andy Costello is personal advisor to the President in the newly created office of Social and Technological Engineering."

Gallin scratched her head. "So Peter Romano advises Andy Costello, who advises the president?"

"You'd think so at first sight. But when we dug a little deeper we found that not only were the president and Peter Romano at university together at Columbia, they were also very close friends and, until a year before they graduated, members of just about every left wing club they could join up to. More interesting still, when Romano founded Cognition, Costello was *his* personal assistant. He spent a year with the company and then graduated suddenly to White House advisor. Now he is part of the president's permanent team."

I said, "So Costello is simply Romano's man in the Oval Office."

"Yes."

I sat forward, set my empty glass on the floor and rested my elbows on my knees.

"OK, let me get this straight in my head. Colonel James Gordon is Military Intelligence attaché at the American Embassy in Madrid. According to the guy who tried to kill me in Paris, he is also General Pat O'Connor's go-between with the Russian Mafia in the south of Spain. According to him there is a secret cooperation between the US and the Russian Mafia."

Marshal nodded. "We all know that you have a budget for black operations which is in excess of a trillion dollars. That money has to come from somewhere, and much of it comes from the CIA's dealings with Mexican cartels, Afghan poppy growers and Russian organized crime."

I gave him a fat-free smile. "I am aware of that. I am part of what they spend that trillion dollars on. According to my informant, one of their key meeting places is Marbella, because the Spanish authorities are easy to bribe.

"So, Colonel James Gordon is General Pat O'Connor's liaison officer with the Russian Mafia in Marbella. Now he has booked a trip to Andorra, where he will be staying at the Grand Continental."

"Precisely, and he booked that trip immediately following Mira Finn's death."

"Meanwhile Boris Semenov, CEO of Anglo-American Armaments, where General Pat O'Connor is a consultant, will also be a guest there, as will Peter Romano, college buddy of the president's and former employer of the president's advisor on social and technological engineering."

"That is correct."

I stood and ran my fingers through my hair, feeling

suddenly my brain was going to explode. "Why would the president of the United States conspire to allow the Russians to nuke our principal cities and the capitals of our closest allies? What possible benefit could that bring to him personally? I mean, aside from anything else, he would die in the strike on DC."

"He is not in DC, Alex. I'm sorry. He is at the newly constructed Camp Evaro, in the mountains above Wye, in the Lolo National Forest in Montana."

"Jesus... What about O'Connor?"

"I don't know. He's gone off the radar."

"How can a thing like this happen?"

"It's a good question. Partly, I'd say, the madness of one man can become infectious."

I grunted. Reluctantly I had to agree with him.

"How come you know so much about this?"

He annoyed me by smiling at Gallin before answering me. "All of America's allies are scrambling like rats on a sinking ship, trying to make some sense of what is happening. Your own department of the Five Eyes is in frantic discussions with the other members, and we are sharing information at an unprecedented rate. I have to say, Israel, who have unique access to American intelligence, have been very cooperative because, as you can imagine, this affects Israel as much as it affects anyone else. If this goes down, we are looking at a catastrophic change in...," he hesitated a moment, "that much over-used phrase, the World Order. If the West implodes, Israel is left suddenly facing the combined madness of fundamentalist Islam, alone."

I stood at the window looking out at the gray sky and the wet streets, with their bobbing umbrellas like mechanized jellyfish. Each one a nucleus of hopes, anxieties, aspirations, thinking about lovers, husbands, wives, children, careers, exams. Not one of them aware of the cataclysm that was about to strike.

What had Oppenheimer said when they tested the first atom bomb? He had quoted from the Bhagavad Gita. I echoed his words aloud without thinking: "Now I am become death, the destroyer of worlds."

Gallin was watching me. She said, "What do you want to do?"

I sighed and turned to look at her. "We have no time. We have to go to Andorra, we have to round up these bastards, beat confessions out of them and take them to DC and have them tell their stories. And we have to find a way to ensure this never happens again."

Marshal gave a small laugh. "I agree, that is precisely what you need to do. But one step at a time. How do you plan to abduct these three men? They will have extremely tight security. And don't forget, you'll have to get them out of Andorra and then Europe, before you get them *in* to the USA."

I shook my head. "I have no idea. We need to get there, case the joint, and then formulate a very fast, simple plan."

He nodded. "All right. Anything I can do to help, let me know. Right now you need some luggage, and to change your appearance sufficiently not to draw attention. I suggest you deal with your hair and moustache while Aila pops out to the Corte Ingles superstore and gets a couple of suitcases, clothes and toiletries. Meantime I'll see what I can dig out in the way of useful toys for you."

"That would be great," I said, wondering why I felt hostile toward him.

Gallin stood. "OK, I'll go get this stuff. Kit, your intel must include what rooms these guys are in, right?"

"Suites, yes."

"You happen to have a plan of the hotel?"

He smiled. "I assumed you'd want one, I've printed a couple for you. But they seem to have use of a hunting lodge somewhere too. Unfortunately we have no intel on that as yet."

She punched him softly on the shoulder. "You da best. Good man."

She stepped toward the door and stopped, turned back and pointed at me.

"Pink shirts, right? Half a dozen? Red and green checkered slacks, and shorts with Luke Skywalker and Superman on them. Anything I didn't think of?"

"Yeah," I said, and wondered why, "don't forget to get yourself a black lace negligee, and pink frilly panties."

I was pleasantly surprised to see her blush, turn and walk away. Moments later the door slammed.

There was something knowing about Kit Marshal's smile. He gestured toward the door. "Bathroom is that way, at the end of the hall on the right. I have left everything you'll need there: hair dye, moustache, glue, heavy glasses. Anything you need just let me know. No doubt Aila will get you appropriate clothes."

"Thanks. No doubt."

I made for the door, but he stopped me.

"Alex." I stopped and turned. "Aila and I have known

each other for many years. There was never anything, on my part or hers. Just professional respect."

I frowned. "Why are you telling me that?"

"Because I am very good at reading people. And I got the impression it would matter to you."

I smiled. "Not at all. But thanks for the thought."

I made my way down the long corridor thinking he was a pretty good guy after all. The English upper class can seem distant and stuck up sometimes, but he was OK. By the time I started putting goo in my hair, I was smiling to myself and humming.

ELEVEN

It was a six-and-a-half-hour drive that took us south as far as Logroño and Zaragoza, and then up through Lleida, back into the Pyrenees. It was a long way around, but it was quicker than driving through the mountains. It rained all the way, so all the way we were driving through a mist of spray. But the worst part was the final stretch through the mountains. It was a slow crawl among hairpin bends, through fog that was sometimes so dense you could barely see twelve feet in front of the hood. At other times it was like a huge cave made of cobwebs that hung in misty strands among the branches of the pine trees.

Darkness came on quickly, and after we had passed the small airport of Seu d'Urgell on our left, some ten miles from Andorra, we began to see scattered snowdrifts among the fog in the fields, among the trees and piled along the roadsides. It looked eerie, shrouded in the trailing billows of mist.

Our six-and-a-half-hour drive wound up being more like

eight hours by the time we finally crossed the border at Sant Juliá de Llória. By then we had risen above the fog, but the snowdrifts had grown larger and deeper under the ice-cold, dark blue sky, in which the stars were encrusted like small slivers of ice.

The border cops pretty much ignored us and waved us through, which bode well for my disguise. Then it was a twenty-minute drive into the nocturnal hills. Here the peaks were covered in thick, white mantles which reflected not just the dark blue of the sky, but the starlight and the yellow light of the rising moon. It was a beautiful and haunting sight which prompted Gallin twice to stop and climb out and gaze at the landscape. The second time I got out with her and we stood in silence, companionably breathing clouds of condensation. All she said was, "We will only live this once," and she stared up into my face. "It will never be like this again."

I didn't argue. I knew what she meant.

We finally arrived at the Sport Hotel Hermitage, in the village of Soldeu, at ten PM. The hotel was nestled in a narrow valley, and as I climbed from behind the wheel I looked up at the huge, dark mass of the mountainside across the river to the south of us. At the very top you could see the winking lights of the Grand Continental five-star hotel. It may have been my imagination, but I thought there was something sinister about it. It looked too aloof, to private, too privileged.

I grabbed our cases from the trunk and followed Gallin through the big glass doors into the polished pine reception. We checked in and were shown to our room by a bellboy who extorted twenty euros from me for opening the curtains and showing us where the bathroom was.

When he was gone Gallin opened the suitcases and threw an evening suit at me, complete with wing collar and dickey-bow tie. "It's the style my father wears, and he is one of the most elegant men I know. The bowtie is a double-ender, I'm afraid, but you just can't get single-enders anymore. At least it's not pre-tied."

I was examining my blond hair and pencil moustache in the mirror, practicing various rictus with my mouth, when she pulled a dark mauve satin offence to morality from her case. There was less cloth on the dress than there were empty spaces. It was low at the back, low at the front, and had at outrageous gash from the ankle all the way up to the hip.

"You're not going to wear that."

Her eyebrows made for the crown of her head. "Why not?"

"Because there is not enough of it to wear. A Brazilian bikini has more cloth on it than that."

She held it up to her body, arched an eyebrow and spoke in a French accent. "Does it meck you want me, chéri?"

I turned away. "No. You're like a brother to me."

"Asshole. Tonight we dine here, but we go for after-dinner drinks at the Grand Continental. I hope that Colonel James Gordon will appreciate me a little more than you do."

I had difficulty answering. I carried my new suit to the bathroom and changed. When I emerged she was barely wearing her dress and gave me a couple of twirls and a wink. If I had been wearing a sphygmomanometer it would have exploded, but I kept my cool by saying, "You realize it's snowing."

We had a light supper and at shortly after eleven, having wrapped Gallin in a woolly shawl, we drove up the hill toward the very grand, Grand Continental.

"How can we be sure they'll be in the bar?" I asked her. "And what if they are? What are we going to do? We haven't thought this through, Gallin. We have no plan. We can't just turn up, beat them up and..."

She watched me a moment. "No third up? Shame, it was working for you. But you can't always have a plan, Mason. Sometimes you have to develop the plan as you go. You're walking down a narrow alley, you're in uniform and you're armed. It's a cold night and your partner stops to take a leak. You keep strolling slowly, thinking he'll catch up. Next thing four guys come at you with knives. Behind you, you hear your partner getting his throat cut. You put your Tav to your shoulder to shoot and you see that one of the four guys can't be more than fourteen. You have no plan. What do you do?"

"Jesus, Gallin." We had arrived at the hotel. I parked beside the sweeping steps to the glass doors where warm light was spilling out and touching the snow. I killed the engine and looked at her. "That happened to you?"

"It lives with me. Part of me. Like my arms and legs. First time I killed someone."

"You killed the kid?"

It wasn't judgmental. No one can pass judgment on a thing like that. But she shook her head. "I killed the three guys and kicked the kid's ass." She shrugged. "But what does that mean? Maybe I killed him seven years later and I don't even know it. Makes you a bit of an existentialist. Point is, sometimes there is no time for plans."

She climbed down and clung to my arm, shivering under

the clear, icy sky as we made for the door. "I was once talking to a very drunk Irish woman," \she went on. "She must have been well in her eighties. She was very erudite and well-bred, and completely langered."

"Langered?"

"Drunk. She told me, 'Aila, sometimes you just have to be Irish, because there is no time to be Greek.'"

I laughed. "What did she mean?"

"I have no idea, but I am pretty sure she was right." And then, after a shrug, "Sometimes there is no time for syllogisms. Major and minor premises and logical inference. Sometimes you just have to roll up your sleeves, wade in and may the Devil take the hindmost."

I nodded. "I know a few Irish scholars who might tell you your friend had it the wrong way round."

The bar was crowded when we got there. Most of the tables were taken and there were waiters in white jackets swooping effortlessly back and forth like house martens, with trays balanced effortlessly on the tips of their upturned wings.

Gallin pulled her cell from her purse and showed me a picture. It was of a thick-set, bull-necked man with a small nose and a big chin. He had short gray hair and the kind of eyes that will coolly assess the convenience or inconvenience of death.

"That's our friend?"

"Courtesy of the Institute."

I led the way to a table and as I removed her shawl I saw him. He was sitting at a table with two other men. One was very tall and vaguely shapeless, with wispy white hair framing a shiny, bald face. He had pink lops and cruel, bulging eyes. I figured he was Semenov because he looked white Russian, where the other guy looked Italian. The other guy was wearing a tastelessly expensive double-breasted suit and a wide, colorful tie. He had a face like an insult and exquisitely tailored black hair. The third man at the table was Colonel James Gordon. He was in a gray suit and he was looking at Gallin with an expression that made me feel oddly violent. He said something and the other two looked at her as she sat. Then they laughed.

She smiled at me. "Looks like we made contact, without a plan."

"I could strike up a conversation with them, if you like. I could go over and ask them what the hell they're looking at."

"I didn't have you down as a jealous man, darling."

"Don't be ridiculous," I said and signaled the waiter. While I did that she turned and smiled at the colonel. I turned back to her. "So what do you suggest we do now? Go back to the colonel's room for a party, beat them senseless and smuggle them to the nearest airfield?"

"We only need one of them. Ideally the colonel."

"We are *not* going to his room for a party!"

"Stop being childish. We have no time and we have to improvise. We focus on their weakest point and we exploit it." She smiled sweetly, leaned forward and laughed like I had said something funny and she just *adored* me. "When I say," she said, "get up and go to the john."

"You're not serious."

"I am serious."

The waiter arrived and I told him two dry martinis. When he'd gone she said, "Now. Go to the john."

Again I felt unreasonably angry, got up and went in

search of the restrooms, trying not to look as though I was in a huff. When I returned five minutes later Colonel James Gordon was sitting in my chair. His expression when he looked up at me was one of amused insolence. He didn't get up. I smiled at him and then at Gallin.

"Darling," she said, "this fascinating man is Colonel James Gordon. James, this is my husband, Bruce. The colonel was telling me all about Madrid. He works at the embassy there."

I smiled like a jealous husband, which I found worryingly easy, and asked, "So, how did you two meet?"

The colonel chortled. "I had better give you your chair back, Bruce, before you get the wrong idea." He stood. He had piggy blue eyes. "I thought I recognized your lovely wife from a visit to Hawaii last year."

I nodded. "And did you?"

He arched an eyebrow at me. "No."

I gestured at his table. "Won't you join us? Then you two can continue discussing Madrid and Hawaii."

"Thanks. I'm afraid we can't. But I have asked Jo to join us tomorrow for cocktails," he paused just long enough to make it insulting, then added, "if you're free, of course."

"We'll be here. Thanks," I pointed at my chair, "for the chair."

He chortled, ravaged Gallin with a special look and prowled back to his table. I sat and sipped my drink. Gallin was smiling at me. "What's up with you, Mason?"

"You mean Bruce."

"OK, what is wrong with you, Bruce?"

"I loved the way you gave the name that special hint of contempt."

"Again, what the hell is wrong with you?"

"Nothing. I am giving it a hint of realism. A man with a wife who goes out undressed, displaying all her virtues for all to see, and virtually throws herself at unknown men—a man with such a wife is a jealous, bitter, sarcastic man. That is the part I am playing. If I were not permanently, pathetically, on the verge of a jealous huff, they would become suspicious."

"Oh, OK."

But her eyes were curious and said she didn't really believe me. I tended to agree with her. They got up, waved to us and left, laughing quietly amongst themselves. I grinned at Gallin to show it really was all an act and toasted.

"Cheers! You look ravishing, by the way."

She raised her glass to me. "About time," she said.

"So seriously," I said as I set my glass down, "what is the plan? I mean, OK, we have seen them and we have met the colonel. He obviously wants to eat you with French fries and we are meeting them tomorrow, but where has that got us? Now we need a plan."

"Well, you see, if you hadn't been so hostile and territorial he might have told you the same thing he told me?"

"What was that?"

"The hunting season ended on the last day of February, small game, boar and deer. But friend Boris, clearly suffering acutely under Western sanctions, has a lodge outside Ansalonga."

Which Marshal told us about."

Precisely. It's called Casa Semenov and is set in a couple of hectares on the banks of the River Sornás, where they sometimes hunt out of season, coz they be bad boyz. And tomorrow he and Gordon are going up there with friend

Romano to do some bad boy hunting. Gordon asked me if I wanted to go along tomorrow morning. I told him I would love to, but I wasn't sure what time we'd get there." She reached in her purse and pulled out a paper napkin with scrawls on it. "So he drew me a map."

"That's good. That's very good."

"Yeah, it just leaves us with the question of how do we take him down. He's built like an ox on steroids."

"See? I knew you were drawn to him."

"What can I say? He's so dense he affects gravity. We need to get there before they do, we need to get eyes on the lodge, and we need to follow them to the hunting ground. Otherwise we will have no idea of where they are in the grounds. Two hectares of snow and mountain forest is a lot of ground to cover."

"OK, and once we are there and we have followed them, what do we do? They will be armed and very dangerous. We need to overpower them, transport them to a vehicle, transport them to a flight and take them to some place, we don't really know where. Not DC."

She nodded and sat a moment pushing her lip out at her drink. She sat back in her chair, regarding my face, and sighed. "I need to talk to Nero."

"What?"

"It can't be avoided. I have to talk to Nero and agree on a place where we can take these guys—or at least the colonel."

"That is very risky. We don't know if he is being bugged. Hell, we don't know if he's been arrested as a way to get to me!"

"I know." She nodded again. "Still, I don't see any other way. We factor in the risks and deal with them as they arise.

But it's a step we need to take. Otherwise," she shrugged and spread her hands, "say we manage to abduct them, like you said—what do we do with them? We *need* to agree on a place with Nero. It could be here. It could be Boris's lodge. And Nero could send ODIN agents to get us."

I sighed. "I'd rather your people came and took us."

She shook her head. "One thing is helping us. Another is actually harboring an American agent on the run. And even if they did, where would they take us? At some point we have to go back to Nero."

"OK." I nodded. "You'd better make the call."

"I'll call from the car. Meantime, our preferred option is they come and get us here in Andorra, to some secure location like a cabin or a lodge. Failing that, some location in Spain or France, close to the border. Failing that..."

"Failing that let him suggest somewhere."

"OK." She jerked her chin at my glass. "You done?"

"Yeah, let's go."

TWELVE

On the way back down the hill I handed her the cell Nero had given me. I hadn't used it, but this now seemed the right time. She called. She called several times, but she got no reply, which scared me because that was unheard of. After agonizing for a full fifteen seconds I gave her Lovelock's number. If Nero was unavailable, Lovelock was always available. There was no reply there, either.

"Shit, Mason. Has there been a palace coup? Have they been arrested?"

"Call your father. He must have his ear to the ground. He must have heard something."

She called her father and put it on speaker.

"Hey Dad."

"Have you made progress?"

"Some. But we have a problem."

"Be quick."

"We're trying to contact Allfather."

I frowned at her. She shrugged. He said, "He has gone

off the radar. ODIN has vanished. There is no trace. In fact there is total silence coming out of DC."

"We need to get a message to him."

"I can't help you. All I can do is contact you as soon as we know anything."

They hung up and she sat staring at the luminous discs of the headlamps sliding down the narrow blacktop ahead of us.

"What the hell do we do now?"

"He has either gone into hiding or he has been arrested. If we try and find him we will either jeopardize him or we'll jeopardize ourselves. Or both."

She nodded. "So we have to go ahead and get the evidence. Once we have it, we assess the situation and decide what to do."

"You mean put off the decision until we have no choice."

She glanced at me. "One thing at least, we are still alive."

I nodded. "I just wish I knew whether the strike had been stopped or postponed. If it's been stopped, why the hell has he gone AWOL?"

"And Colonel Gordon is still at large, looking smug."

I drove on in silence for a couple of minutes. As we neared the hotel and I slowed to park I said, "Gallin. It's not too late for you to pull out."

"Shut up, Mason. This is everyone's fight. And something else; this is something my dad taught me. You don't win in this life by abandoning the people you care about when they are in need. You stick together, even when everything is lost. You stick together."

I sighed and shook my head. "You shouldn't say things like that."

She scowled at me. "Why not?"

"Not dressed like that."

"Aw shuddup!" She punched me in the arm and climbed giggling from the car.

In the bedroom she closed the door and began to strip, speaking urgently as she did so.

"OK, decision: Do we go before dawn and find a location near the lodge, or do we go tonight, break into the lodge and wait for them?"

I went and stood gazing out the window at the glistening lights in the snowy landscape.

"The place will have an alarm system, probably a very sophisticated one. It probably has a backup generator too, in case of power outages."

I heard a zipper and a rustle of cloth.

"OK, you can turn around now, Prudence."

I did, she was in jeans and a plaid shirt. I said, "Question: is Boris going home tonight, or is he going to stay here till the morning?"

She dropped into an armchair. "That's a good question. My gut feeling, and that's all I've got, is that they had a lot to talk about. Either they were all going back to his pad, or they were all staying here."

"And why go back if they have everything they need right here?"

"That's my feeling."

"OK, so here's what we do. We don't bother with the lodge. We wait for them on the road outside the main gate, ambush them and..."

I faltered. We stared at each other a moment and I sighed and ran my fingers through my hair. Ambush them how?

With two semi-automatics? Aside from being totally ineffectual, we needed them alive. And the problem remained, once ambushed, what the hell did we do with them?

"Let's get a couple of hours' sleep," I said. "Four AM we get a flask of coffee from room service and make our way to the lodge. We find a way to jump them when they arrive and take it from there."

"That's your plan?"

"It's the best I can do on what we have."

She shrugged and grinned. "It's a pretty good plan, Bruce."

We slept for three hours, then rose, had a cold shower each and dressed for the snow. Gallin called down for a flask of coffee and some hot croissants and by four AM we were pulling out of Soldeu on the G2, going north and west. The sky had become overcast and once outside of town the darkness was dense. It had snowed and there was a film of ice and snow on the blacktop, so I had to drive slow just to keep from sliding into the drifts.

At Canillo I cut off the main road and took the CS240, a narrow, secondary road that wound up the mountainside in a series of tight hairpin bends. Everything was black, except for the small pool of amber light cast by the headlamps, sweeping back and forth across the trees and the slightly luminous snowdrifts.

The descent was longer than the climb. It seemed to go on forever, winding and bending back and forth, with the big tires drifting on the sludge on the road surface. It was a fifteen-mile drive, but it took more than half an hour.

Eventually, following Gallin's rudimentary map, we came to the town of Ordino, and we knew that the hamlet of Sornas was just half a mile ahead. When we got there we almost missed it in the dark. It was a small cluster of houses, half concealed among the densely packed pines, and a narrow road that wound through them. It skirted the base of a mountain and then buried itself in black forest along the bottom of a ravine. We followed into the impenetrable darkness and gradually began to climb. Gallin said:

"You should kill the lights. There might be somebody at the lodge."

I switched off the headlamps and we ground, painfully slow, up the black snake of the road until we emerged from the trees into a clearing. Ahead on the right there was an iron gate. On the left trees swarmed up a slope, their bases enveloped in heavy drifts.

I continued slowly up the hill while Gallin jumped down and ran for the gate. There was a sign on it. Through the windshield I saw her read it, then turn and give me the thumbs up.

I went on a little farther until I was out of sight, came off the road and killed the engine, then I went back to join Gallin, who was looking up the slope at the snow and the trees, with slow billows of condensation escaping from her mouth like fleeing ghosts.

"I'm having a crazy idea," I told her. "It really is a stupid idea, but I think it might just work."

"Yeah? At least you have an idea. All I can think of is you on one side of the road, me on the other and we shoot the bastards. But that won't help your cause much. Plus they will have hunting rifles, and two of them at least know how to use them."

I shook my head. Stamped my feet and billowed. "No, we have to make snowballs."

"Snowballs..."

"Yeah."

She bent double, giggling with her hands between her knees. "You're right. That is a really stupid idea. And no, it won't work."

"No, you don't understand. I mean, *snowballs!* Three and four feet across, compact, four, five or six of them here, forming a barrier blocking the road." I pointed ten or fifteen feet down the road, just before the turnoff for the gate. "And another five or six or seven up there, up the slope among the trees. When the car slows to a stop because of the barrier, we let them roll at the back of the car. They will block the road and the car won't be able to move backward or forward. They won't be able to see in this weather whether it was a small avalanche or a series of snowballs. They will get out to clear the way, and then we take them. Small arms will be more than enough. If we have to we shoot Semenov and Romano—that will be enough to make Gordon behave."

She came over close and stared hard at my chest. She spoke quietly. "That is creative." She sounded quite serious. "Using your environment, your circumstances, to your advantage." Her eyes flicked up to my face. "That's really good, Mason. I mean it."

"Um..."

"OK, don't hang around staring. Let's do it."

We scrambled up the hill and started making small, compact snowballs which we rolled back and forth in the deep snow, until they were three and four feet in width. Then we pressed and patted them until they were dense and compact, and then we rolled them some more, just like we were making snowmen. It was easier than I had expected, and after about an hour we had a barrier of eight large balls of snow cutting off the narrow road from the bend where the gate was, and we had ten more of them positioned up the slope, concealed by the trees, roughly where the rear of the vehicle would be when they arrived.

It was only then that we began seriously to consider the fact that we didn't know at what time they were going to arrive. It was very cold, and so far the exercise and the activity had kept us warm. But now the work was done, there was a limit to how long we could stay out here doing nothing.

I checked my watch. It was six fifteen AM, but there was no sign of the dawn yet. Gallin said, "We wait in the Range Rover. We'll see the glow from their headlamps if they come before the dawn. If they come after the dawn we will have frozen to death anyway, so it won't matter."

"Didn't they give you some idea of what time they'd be here?"

We clambered in the truck, shivering, and slammed the doors. I put on the heating. She nodded. "Yeah, he said they were going to have breakfast here and go out to hunt after breakfast."

I looked out at the blackness. "Three hours max."

"Meantime we can play I Spy."

At six thirty she said, "I spy with my little eye, something beginning with G, G."

"Gorgeous guy?"

"No, ghostly glow."

She pointed behind me and I turned to see a ghostly

luminescence rising above the hill and making spindly stencils out of the pine trees.

"OK! Let's go!"

We scrambled and ran from the Range Rover up through the trees, wading against the deep drifts of snow, billows of condensation freezing against our lips and cheeks as we ran. We reached the top of the hill and took up our positions. I glanced at Gallin and was suddenly overwhelmed by a sense of the absurdity of what we were doing, and the impossibility of its success. She must have read my expression because she whispered hoarsely, "It's crazy, but the car will be stranded and they will have to get out. It'll work!"

We waited five minutes and soon we heard the whine of a car driving in low gear, and a few moments later the amber glow of the headlamps appeared, washing against the far bank of the road. A sudden twist of anxiety gripped me. I turned to Gallin and rasped, "*This is insane! We don't even know if it's them!*"

"*Shut up!*"

"*What?*"

"*Shut! Up!*"

The Audi SUV appeared around the bend, moving at maybe twenty miles per hour. Its headlamps picked out the barrier of snow we had erected and gradually came to a halt with the hood three or four feet from it. I confess I hesitated a second until Gallin hissed savagely at me, "*Now! Damn it, Mason! Now!*" and we both heaved. The huge balls of snow, frozen hard now, bounded down the slope, gathering more snow as they went, and thundered into a huge cascade against the back of the vehicle, wedging against the wheels and forming a dense wall of ice and snow around the trunk. Any attempt to back out of it would immobilize the car.

We didn't wait. We ran and scrambled down the slope, dodging the trees and slipping and sliding in the snow. We arrived at the bottom of the slope level with the rear of the vehicle, just as the three men were emerging from it. Two from the front and one from the rear. They stopped and stared at us as we pulled our weapons.

For a moment it was impossible to make out who they were. But as we approached their faces came into focus and I smiled. It was Gordon, Romano and, on the far side of the vehicle, Semenov. So far at least it was working to plan.

Gallin spoke, "All right boys, let's all stay real calm and everything is going to work out dandy. This is the Andorra Park Rangers Office, and we heard you boys were hunting out of season." Before they could answer she jerked her chin at the long, willowy form of Semenov. "You, Lanky, get your skinny ass around this side of the vehicle."

"You out of your mind. I am not going to obey your orders. I am get back in car and fuck you!"

He moved toward the car. There was a loud crack and Gallin's muzzle flashed. Semenov whiplashed and I saw a dark plume of gore spray from the back of his head. He did a kind of swaying wobble and thudded into the snow.

She didn't falter. "Anybody else want to test the resolve of the Andorra Park Rangers?"

They had both gone very still. So we had reached that part of the plan where we would "take it from there" or "cross that bridge when we got to it." Well, there we were and I had no idea what to do next. My mouth started to speak on its own.

"Ranger Joanna, bring the vehicle while I cover Sergeant Rock and Banana Nose Maldonado here."

She sprinted away up the road and Gordon growled. "You two. I might have known. You're Alex Mason. Pat warned me."

"Shoulda listened to Uncle Pat, Jimmy. Now, come a little closer, lace your fingers and put your hands on your head. Now you, Romano, get on your knees and take his bootlaces out."

He'd undone them and pulled them out by the time Gallin reversed the Range Rover to the lodge gate. She jumped down and started burying Semenov in the snow.

"Now," I told Romano, "tie his wrists behind his back with one of the laces. Give the other lace to me. And Romano, if when I check it, it's loose, I am going to tell Ranger Joanna, and she is going to be real mad at you. We all know what that means, right?"

"Yeah, cut the ranger shit, will you? I'm cute. I'll tie it tight."

He tied them tight enough to make Gordon curse. I waved the gun at the truck and snarled, "OK, quick march. Gordon, you climb in the back, but leave your boots in the snow. You, Romano, you take your laces out and give them to Ranger Joanna."

As we approached the Range Rover Gordon removed his boots and Gallin shoved him in the back. Then she tied Romano's wrists, took his boots and shoved him in the back too. I gave her the spare lace so now she had two. She stuffed them in her pocket, clambered in the front passenger seat and snarled, "First bastard who moves loses his knees. C'mon, Ranger Bruce, let's go!"

I fired up the engine, swung it round, put it in reverse and rammed the gate with the trunk. There was a horrible sound of tortured metal, but the gates busted open and we rolled through. While Gallin pushed the gates closed again, I turned the Range Rover around. She clambered in, grinned at me with excessive enthusiasm, and we roared up the hill toward the lodge. I had no idea what I was doing, but at least I was doing something.

Though even as that thought passed through my mind, and as the dark bulk of the lodge appeared ahead of me with gabled roofs and tall chimneys, the way ahead started to become clear.

I smiled. it would not be pretty, but it would work.

THIRTEEN

THE LODGE WAS A MASSIVE, THREE-STOREY PILE with black slate roofs, turrets and tall chimney pots. The blacktop drive led to a large circle in front of the main doors that was flanked by cypress and pines. Broad stone steps swept to a stone porch inside which were the doors. The trees and the steps were shrouded with crisp snow, as were the black slate roofs, where it had drifted against the chimney pots.

We got down and dragged Gordon and Romano from the back seat. The ground was cold and they did a kind of barefoot chicken dance, with their knees high in the air to the front door of the lodge. There Gallin pulled a bunch of keys from her pocket and grinned at me.

"Semenov's. He didn't look like he was going to be using them any time soon."

She unlocked the door and shoved Gordon and Romano inside. We were in a broad hall with a staircase climbing the rear wall from right to left. There were two doors in the wall on the left and another two in the wall on the right. I closed the main door behind me and snapped, "Office!"

Gordon whipped round and frowned at me, but Romano had already started making his way to the near door on the right. Gallin opened it and glanced inside, then stood back for Romano and Gordon to enter.

The room was old-world luxury, with paneled walls, floor-to-ceiling redwood bookcases, heavy red Wilton carpet wall-to-wall and antique leather sofas and armchairs. There was a cold fireplace and beside it a huge, heavily engraved desk with a computer on it.

I said, "Lie facedown, both of you." Gordon began to say something. I cut him short. "Me, personally, I'd like to keep both of you alive. I think you might be useful. My friend Ranger Jo isn't so bothered about that. She says as long as we have some kind of recording of one of you, that should be enough. So, my advice to both of you is, don't upset Ranger Jo. Don't give her an excuse. Because I have to say I find her very hard to control."

He sighed and grunted and got down on his knees. Gallin put her boot on his shoulder and gave him a little shove. He screwed up his face and went down with an ugly thud. Over to one side Romano had managed to get himself down by supporting himself against the desk. The last few inches were still hard.

When they were both uncomfortably on the floor I sat myself on one of the big leather armchairs and started to speak.

"OK, gentlemen, this is the situation. I, as you know, am

Alex Mason. I have no problem telling you this because General Pat O'Connor already knows it."

"No shit," the colonel growled. I ignored him and went on. "Now here's the thing. My career, and my life, both of which I would like to keep, depend on one of you gentlemen explaining to me right now how Russian agents managed to find out that Mira Finn was in Paris to collect Dr. Rusenko. I know you will be reluctant to tell me, but believe me, when I am motivated I can be so convincing it makes Ranger Jo's eyes water."

They both remained quiet.

"Colonel, I know you are the general's go-between with the Russian mob and the elements of the federal government. We know that your position as Military Intelligence attaché at the American Embassy in Madrid made you ideal for the job because of the Russian Mafia's presence in Marbella. I don't need to prove you have the information I need. I know you have it. I just need to persuade you to give it to me."

I sighed, smiled and turned to Romano. "Peter Romano, the ultimate gray man. You own sixty percent of Cognition, a publicity and social media company in DC. But you don't get involved in the day-to-day administration of the company. You leave that to your partner, Abraham Gold, and your gang of Ivy League psychologists. You don't waste your time on that. No, you consult for a small group of corporate giants in the field of IT and social media; and for one Andy Costello in particular, a personal advisor to the president in the newly created Office of Social and Technological Engineering." I paused. "But your relationship with the president actually goes quite a bit deeper than that, doesn't it, Romano? In fact, it was you who chose Costello for that job, wasn't it? Because you and President Jed Benoi go back a long way, don't you?

"Not only were you at university together at Columbia, you were actually buddies hanging out at all the most fashionable left-wing clubs. Costello is your man in the Oval Office, placed there so you and Jed are not seen to be too close.

"So either one of you can tell me what I need to know. But I figure, to encourage you to talk, what I need to do is have Ranger Jo take Mr. Romano here next door," I looked at her and asked, "Right? So you can play with his sensitive areas for a bit. Meanwhile I'll show Colonel Gordon some of the skills I picked up in Colombia, and then we compare notes to see who is lying. And *that* guy gets to stay in Andorra, with the very cool Boris Semenov."

Gallin frowned at me. "The skills you picked up in Colombia?" She shook her head. "I told you I want no part of that."

I sighed and stared at the ceiling for a moment. "Don't get squeamish on me now. This is *not* the time."

"I *told* you I don't want any part of that, Alex!" Her cheeks flushed and her eyes were bright. "That is *not* who we are!"

My voice began to rise. "I bow to your superior morality, but frankly, I don't see we have much choice. You get to go back home, while I get quietly shot in a back street." I pointed at Romano with my weapon. "And these guys are *not* going to talk without some serious persuasion!"

Tears were starting in her eyes. "Then we waterboard them, Mason!"

"It is *not enough!* These guys are committed up to their necks!"

She was practically hysterical. "All right! We use pliers! But for Christ's sake, Mason! I want to come out of this with my humanity intact!"

I yelled at her, gripping her shoulders in my hands and shaking her. "*Listen to me! Listen to me! We-have-no-choice! It's that or I die! Do you understand?*"

She wrenched away from me and stormed over to the desk, like she might find some salve there for her conscience. She stood a moment in silence, then turned savagely toward me, pointing a trembling finger at my face, like a gun.

"All right, Mason! We do it your way. But I am going on record as having opposed this! And when they court marshal you for the obscenity you are about to commit, know that I *will* testify against you."

We stared at each other for a long moment. Then I turned and grabbed Romano by his collar.

"Come on! On your feet!"

I dragged him up and he started thrashing and screaming, babbling incoherently. I shoved him toward the door and shouted, "*Shut up!*"

I turned and threw the two remaining bootlaces at Gallin. "Tie up his ankles, if you don't feel too sorry for him. And remember, for Christ's sake, if it ain't hurting he ain't telling the truth!"

I pushed Romano through the door and out into the hallway. There I stopped him and pointed the Sig at his head and said, "Sit on the floor."

He was trembling badly, sweating and weeping.

"Mr. Mason, I swear I will tell you anything, do

anything, this is really not necessary. I am..." His lips got stuck on *m* and for a moment all he could say was "Mmmm, I'm mmm," as he slid down the wall to the floor.

"What?"

"I'm a very pragmatic man, I do not like pain, I can't, not torture, I swear, whatever you want to know, I am well connected, I can tell you almost anything."

I shook my head. "No, you see, I have to be *sure*. I have to know that you know that I am *serious*."

"I just saw, saw, saw...Boris..."

"That was her. She kills people at the drop of a hat. But she is squeamish about..." I stared deep into his eyes. "About pain. I am not bothered by pain. If it's hurting you, it's not hurting me, right? She sees a man weeping and sobbing and begging for death—you see that *a lot* in Colombia and Mexico—she goes to pieces."

"You don't need to do this. I will tell you everything now. It will save time."

Suddenly I went crazy. I screamed in his face, "*You son of a bitch! You think you can lie to me! You think I am stupid? You think I'm some kind of a clown? You think you can play games with me? I am going to skin you alive, you son of a bitch!*" He cowered away and started weeping, and I let out a horrific, mind-bending, blood-curdling scream that tore at my throat and went on and on, weaving pathetically, heart-rendingly, through the octave scales, until it died in a sobbing whimper.

Romano was cowering against the wall, staring at me like I was out of my mind. I took my cell out of my pocket and placed it on the floor beside him.

"Tell it. And believe me, if you try to lie to me, I will peel you like a banana and poor surgical spirits over your nuts."

In the study, Gallin and Gordon had watched me push Romano through the door and slam it behind me. There had been a brief silence in which Gallin had turned to Gordon. She had smiled at him and said, "All right, Colonel, so you figured out I am opposed to torture. A lot of officers are. Don't run away with the idea that that makes me weak. You are facing a court martial for murder and for treason. So you have one chance, just one, to avoid spending the rest of your life behind bars, and that is to talk before—"

And she stopped dead, because they were both staring at the door, through which they could hear me screaming like a maniac. The last words they heard were, "*I am going to skin you alive, you son of a bitch!*"

And then there was the insane, heart-wrenchingly pathetic, blood-curdling scream, which ended in a sobbing whimper. After which she looked at Gordon and told him, "I think you might be too late."

He had swallowed hard, eying the door, and said. "OK, let's just take it easy. What is it exactly you want to know?"

Gallin pulled out her cell and started to record. "Let's start with your relationship with General Patrick O'Connor."

Meanwhile, on my side of the door I had hunkered down in front of Romano with the Sig pressed against his left knee. I told him: "Tell me about your relationship with the president, Peter, and I won't send you to hospital for them to amputate all your limbs."

He nodded. "It looks like the project has fallen through anyway. It should have happened by now."

I pulled out my cell and started to record. "Say that again, and explain what you mean."

"That's why we were at the Grand Continental. The bunker. They have a bunker."

"What?"

"Since the sixties, Andorra has been a favored, secret meeting place for people like us, involved in..."

He hesitated. I said, "Manipulating world affairs?"

"Yeah, I guess. The Grand Continental has always been the go-to place. It was built specifically for those meetings. The rooms are swept for bugs daily, and there is a bunker."

"That's why the Bilderberg Group chose it."

"Of course. And that's why we have this lodge."

"There is a bunker here too?"

"In the basement. Pat was supposed to meet us here. But he didn't show. I'm guessing the plan fell through."

I nodded for a while. "What plan, Peter?"

"It's complicated. Something should have happened by now. I am really scared. You are really scaring me. It's hard for me to think right now."

I smiled. I made sure it was my nice smile. "Try and get a grip, Peter. Right now, Gordon is in there spilling his guts to Ranger Jo."

He winced. "That's not her real name, right?"

For a moment I felt sorry for him. He was a particular type of DC parasite. They live in the apparent inviolable security offered by the Holy Trinity: the White House, the Capitol and the Pentagon, and everything outside of that environment is nasty stuff that happens to other people. And here he was, with nasty stuff happening to him, barefoot and cold in a foreign country.

"No," I said, "that's not her real name. But you don't want to know her real name, because if you do, it means you're going to die. Now get with the program, Pete. Because if he tells her everything, and proves more knowledgeable than you, you get to stay in the Pyrenees keeping company with Boris. So, once again, what plan, Pete?"

He closed his eyes and took a deep breath. "It's really complicated."

"You said that."

"OK, about twenty years ago it was pretty much established that the planet, under optimum conditions, could not sustain more than nine billion people, while sustaining anything like quality of life, even for the elite."

He edged himself into a slightly more comfortable position, propped against the wall.

"I mean, truly, the planet can support maybe one and a half billion people, maximum, using basic technology like plowing, building with bricks, horse-drawn vehicles." He nodded several times. "*One and a half billion!* You know what the world population was this morning?" He didn't wait for a reply. "Seven point nine three four billion, and growing at a rate of three or four people per second. You know how many people have been added to the population this year—we're in March, right? Month number three! Already nearly seventeen million people. And political leaders all over the world wanting to add, add, add! We need more people! More people! To pay taxes, to add to the coffers! But they are blind!"

"What are you telling me, Pete? That you engineered this whole crazy scheme to reduce the population?"

"We are racing to extinction, Mr. Mason! And you

would be surprised to discover how many of the world's most eminent leaders—not political leaders, they are puppets! I am talking about the men who actually make things happen on this planet. You would be surprised to discover how many of them have woken up to the fact that the planet is about to become a living hell if we do not dramatically reduce the population."

"OK, Pete, you made your point. What are you telling me? The president of the United States got together with Putin and Pat O'Connor in a re-run of *One Flew Over the Cuckoo's Nest Goes Nuclear*? Come on, Pete! What are you talking about?"

He shook his head. There was something feverish in his eyes. "No," he said, "you don't understand. Nobody understands. It is not enough to reduce the population. We did that in 1916 and again in 1939; look what happened. It just surged back again. And COVID made no impact at all! No, we have to reduce the population, but we have to *radically change the system* too. So we can maintain stable numbers, so there will be no regeneration."

"Are you telling me the *president* was a party to this madness? Who were the members of this conspiracy?"

He licked his lips and tried to swallow. "I don't know, exactly. Presidents just do what they're told. There are a couple of IT giants, visionaries. General O'Connor is just one of many who have come to realize America is no longer leading the way. There is a desperate need for change..."

"I am going to ask you one last time, Pete. Was the president a party to this?"

He swallowed hard, then slowly nodded.

"Yes."

FOURTEEN

I STOOD AND THOUGHT FOR A MOMENT, WITH THE uncomfortable feeling that the world was collapsing around my ears. I locked the feeling away in a deep dungeon in my unconscious, along with the first day I got hit at school, and the ugly satisfaction I felt when I hit back.

"You say there is a bunker in this place too?"

"Yeah, in the basement. My hands are really hurting. I am cooperating with you. Please..."

"Yeah, give me a minute. So what was your plan? The missiles would strike and then what? You have radioactive clouds over London, Brussels, Berlin and Paris. Western Europe would be uninhabitable for decades, maybe centuries. You weren't going to just crawl into the cellar and stay there."

"No!" He half shouted it. "We were going to fly back to Montana. The prevailing winds will carry the radiation from California down to the south, and from New York and

Washington, out into the Atlantic. The Midwest will be largely untouched.. This would be the new cradle of—"

"Stop. Shut up. Fly back to Montana? How?"

He stared at me for a moment. His face said it was dawning on him that it was all over.

"We have..." He sighed, sagged and looked away from me. "We have a plane prepped to get away."

"Where?"

"About half a mile west of here, through the woods, there is some flat farmland. We made a runway there."

"What the hell are you flying that would get you to Montana?"

"A Bombardier Global 8000. It has a range of almost eight thousand miles. It will get us to the president's ranch, Camp Evaro, above the Lolo National Forest in Montana.."

"Jesus Christ! And the president *knows* this bullshit is going down?"

He shrugged and repeated, "The presidents just do as they're told."

I pushed open the door to the study. Gallin was standing in the middle of the floor, staring at me. I said:

"We need to talk."

She said, "We need to get the hell out of here, fast."

"Why? What's happening?"

"They have a team on the way, from Rota, in Cadiz."

"How? How do they know...?"

"Ask your guy. See if the story matches."

I closed the door, hunkered down and pressed the muzzle of the Sig hard into his knee. "Is there a team on its way?"

He squeezed his eyes tight and started to hyperventilate. "Yes."

"Where from?"

"The American airbase at Rota. We were supposed to check in for an escort. If we didn't they would send a team."

"How long ago?"

"An hour."

"Dammit!" I shouted. "They'll be arriving anytime now!"

I kicked the door open. Gallin was dragging Gordon to his feet. I bellowed, "*We have to go now! Now!*" To Gordon I shouted, "*You straggle, you die! Let's go!*"

Gallin shoved Gordon out as I dragged Romano to his feet. "*Shoes!*" I shouted. "*Get your shoes on!*"

We scrambled out into the freezing pre-dawn. Gallin wrenched open the rear door of the Range Rover and threw out their shoes. As they pulled them on she came up close to me and whispered, "We have the recordings. Do we need them?"

I thought about it. Without them we could move twice as fast. But when we got to the States...

"We haven't even got a plan, Gallin. We can't answer that question because we haven't even got a plan. We need every asset we can get. We hang on to them, for now at least."

"OK." She turned to them. "OK, on your feet! Steady run. Try anything funny and I'll shoot you."

We set off at a jog through the freezing gray air, over sodden lawn, peppered with patches of frozen snow, toward the black line of the woods. Twice Romano slipped and fell, and I had to drag him to his feet. His shoes were loose and his feet were freezing. The second time I pulled him up he was sobbing. For a moment I felt a stab of pity. Whatever kind of rat he was, he was suffering, in fear and in pain. I covered it, from myself as much as from him, by grabbing the scruff of his neck and pushing him forward, snarling, "Be grateful you haven't got radiation raining on you, you son of a bitch!"

We were approaching the tree line when the sound of the choppers reached us, thudding across the fields. "*Drop!*" I shouted, and heard Gallin's echoing shout. We fell to the ground, scrambled round and looked back. I rasped in a whisper, "*Move, twitch, make the smallest sound and you are both dead meat.*"

There were three of them. The came over the horizon, black, menacing, like giant insects silhouetted against the first graying of dawn. They hovered a moment over the lodge, then one headed down toward the gate while the other two settled on the blacktop in front of the house. I said, "*Now!*"

And we ran for the trees, just thirty yards away. Once in there we would lose them. We had a chance.

Then Romano dodged left, spinning on his heels, and started sprinting across the frozen grass, screaming. "*Here! Here! We're over here! They have us! Here! Here!*"

I went after him, cursing violently under my breath. And as I ran I saw three silhouettes run over the rise, maybe a hundred and fifty or two hundred yards away. All three of them had assault rifles and they were all staring at me and Romano. I saw the unmistakable movement as one of the silhouettes put his rifle to his shoulder. Romano was screaming in a crazy, shrill voice, "*Peter Romano! Peter Romano! Don't shoot. Mason is—*"

He stopped dead in his tracks and the back of his head exploded in a shower of spray and gore. Then the report rolled across the field. I had already turned and was running frantically back toward Gallin and Gordon.

I heard Gordon curse. I yelled at him as I ran. *"You'd better pray you get the chance to make a deal with the FBI, Gordon! Right now you are a dead man whichever way you cut it!"*

He didn't answer. He just ran. He knew. We plunged into the trees. Suddenly we were in darkness with visibility of only twelve or fifteen feet ahead. Gordon was fit, but he was also heavy and his shoes, without laces, were an encumbrance to him. He tried a few times to stray to the right or left, but Gallin stayed with him, shoving him occasionally, and repeatedly checking her watch. Pretty soon, after the third time she pointed out the correct direction, I realized she had a compass on her watch. It is not only easy to lose your sense of direction in a forest. It's impossible not to.

Then we heard them behind us: their boots running, tramping through the undergrowth, making no effort to be silent. They didn't need to. We were sitting ducks. All they needed to do was close in. And they were closing in fast. Gallin and I might have made it, but Gordon was slowing us down badly.

Suddenly he made a funny little dance, kicked off his shoes and started to sprint. I snapped to Gallin, *"Can you fly?"*

"Of course I can fly!"

"Keep going. Stay with him! Get the plane and go!"

"Why? What are you...?"

But I was gone. I had a map of the area in my mind and I

sprinted north and west, counting my strides as yards as I went toward where the forest grew more dense and sprawled up the mountainside. When I had reached a hundred strides I stopped, turned, dropped to one knee and emptied my magazine into the trees, shooting south and east where I calculated they would be running.

I didn't hang about for the response. I scrambled to my feet and ran back, aiming for where I figured the airfield had to be. Behind me automatic fire ripped through the woods, tearing at branches and splintering tree trunks. In the cold, wet darkness of the forest I fell, slipped on damp branches, collided with trees and crashed through undergrowth which tore at my face and hands. I tried to do all that quietly, but was not very successful. My wild, desperate hope was that I had managed to lure them off course, if only temporarily. I knew once they stopped shooting they would hear me running. But the source of sound is hard to pinpoint in dense forest. I might just have bought us a few crucial minutes—or seconds.

And then I had broken out into a clearing. I could see another tree line maybe two or three hundred yards away across flat turf. But to my left the mossy grassland stretched away fifty yards toward a large, wooden barn, and outside the barn was a patch of tarmac that stretched into a runway that must have been almost half a mile long. And sitting on that tarmac was an exquisite Bombardier Global 8000, glistening gently in the first rays of the dawning sun.

I was bruised, scratched, exhausted and my lungs were hurting from dragging in frozen air. But I sprinted the sprint of my life. I didn't call or shout, so as not to attract the attention of our pursuers, but the sound of my breathing was thunder in my own ears. Yet, louder than my own breathing was the sudden high-pitched whine of the jet's turbines as it began to slide toward the runway.

In my head I could hear my voice yelling, "*No! No, no, no!*" though I bit back the words and ran harder. I knew Gallin would not leave me willingly. But I had told her to go and she knew the importance of getting the evidence to Nero. We could not afford to have Gordon killed here.

I drove my legs harder, though the muscles were cramping with pain. I was wheezing painfully and shards of agony were stabbing through my lungs. The jet started to taxi toward the runway and behind me I heard the crackle of automatic fire. They were marksmen. I had seen that when they had shot Romano. Now I had the quandary: the shortest distance to the jet was a straight line, but a straight line offered my pursuers the best target.

I was twenty yards, twenty paces from the tail of the jet. A round hit the turf beside me and showered me with damp dirt. I dodged left and saw that the jet was starting to accelerate. Involuntarily I screamed, "*Gallin!*" They had seen us already. It made no difference now if I made a noise.

I was on tarmac. The guns crackled like fireworks behind me. Rounds strafed the blacktop, sending showers of gravel and tar into the air. I was behind the Bombardier. My muscles were failing and I was losing control of my legs. And now I realized, in the hot wash of air, that I was in the direct line of the jet engines, and they would incinerate me in a few seconds as she went for takeoff.

The plane was just fifteen strides away, but moving. I wanted to give up, but I couldn't. A stupid voice in my head told me I had no protocol for that procedure. And as I dragged a final burst from my quivering legs, I saw the hatch open and the steps come down. I ran, stumbling. Behind me I heard shouts. A round spat off the fuselage, another ricocheted off the asphalt by my feet. Ten more paces, but the plane was moving, turning every stride into five. I screamed and roared, demanding more from my body than it could give, and then I had my hand on the rail. I dragged myself another four running strides and clambered onto the steps, shouting and gasping. Hot, searing lead bit into my shoulder. I fell forward. The hatch started to close and the jet started to accelerate.

I fell in a heap into the cabin. The floor lurched underneath me and I slid back toward the seats. Then agony flooded my body.

We climbed and climbed for an eternity into the dome of the sky. Eventually, very slowly, we began to level off and I clawed my way into a sitting position with my back against the wall. There was an intense pain in my shoulder and all down my right arm which was making it hard to think. I managed to struggle to my feet. To my right was the cabin. It was everything you would expect from a luxury private jet: high-gloss wooden tables, leather armchairs and a sofa, a well-stocked bar and a galley kitchen at the rear.

And just a few feet away from me, with raw, bare feet, lying facedown on the carpet was Colonel James Gordon. There was a thin trickle of blood matting his hair just above the base of his skull. He didn't look dead, but he looked like he might want to be when he woke up.

I lurched a couple of steps toward the cockpit, steadied myself on the wall and pulled the door open. Gallin glanced up at me.

"You're alive," she said, without any particular inflection.

"Are you sure?" I lowered myself into the copilot's chair and strapped myself in. "What happened to Gordon?"

"Arithmetic."

"Arithmetic happened to him?"

"There were only two of us and he was a hundred percent bigger than me. Also I had two things to do, guard him and fly the plane. The numbers didn't work."

"So you shot him?"

"No!" Her glance told me to use my brain. Mine told her my brain hurt too much to be used. "I slugged him with the butt of my P226. You're bleeding from your shoulder."

"I knew that."

"Can you fly for ten minutes? I can't put it on auto until we're out over the Atlantic because I want to stay below the radar." I frowned at her. I was feeling like an idiot, but the pain was dulling my mind.

"I need to get the first-aid kit, Mason, for your arm, and I need to secure Gordon. Can you fly the plane?" I nodded. "Just try not to crash into any mountains. OK?"

"I think I can manage that."

She handed over the controls and stood. We had a brief dip, dive and yaw, but after a few seconds I had her back on course for the Bay of Biscay and the Atlantic. I heard a couple of cupboards open and close behind me. Then Gallin's voice told me, "It must be in the galley. I'll get the colonel properly strapped in while I'm at it."

The door opened and closed. The jet was steady. I took a couple of deep breaths and ignored the pain by focusing on the altimeter and the mountains that were giving way to the

Plaines of Aquitaine and Occitan. I watched as the Pyrenees inched away below us and wondered if Semenov had filed a flight plan with the Spanish and French aviation authorities. I struggled to think what I would say if we were challenged. The door opened behind me. I said, "Do you know if Semenov filed a flight plan? What are we going to tell them if they radio us?"

"Tell them if they don't let us through, I will blow Alia Gallin's brains all over the cockpit walls. Tell them that United States Army Colonel James Gordon is in charge of the jet, he has diplomatic immunity and he is transporting a wanted prisoner, Alex Mason, back to the USA."

I turned and looked. He had Gallin in a choke hold with his left arm, and her Sig pointed at her head.

"Be a shame to kill her before tasting her, so stay cool and just do as I say, Mr. Mason. Let's start with take out your weapon and drop it near my feet. Do anything stupid and I will make a real mess of her lovely face."

I pulled out my weapon and carefully dropped it near his feet. He grunted.

"OK, now you, sweet cheeks, sit yourself down in the pilot's seat and get us home to Montana."

She got into the pilot's seat and strapped herself in. Then she jerked her head at me.

"He needs first aid. He's shot in the shoulder. He needs attention right now."

"No kidding." He chuckled an ugly laugh and sat in a fold-down seat behind us. "You know what, Captain Gallin? I don't give a shit. Now pilot and shut up."

FIFTEEN

I AM NOT SURE HOW LONG WE FLEW, BUT I COULD see the ocean beneath us and I was aware I was becoming feverish. I figured we were over the Bay of Biscay, just past Bayonne, and I had slipped into slightly delirious sleep a couple of times, when I became aware of Gallin shouting. When I looked I was surprised to see her on her feet, with no one in the pilot's seat. She had her face real close to Gordon's and was shouting at him.

"Army colonel, right? They teach you to fly in the Army, Gordon? I don't think so! So if you want me to take this damned crate to Montana you'd better get off your ass and bring me the kit so I can fix this man up! Or fly the damned plane yourself!"

He was shouting too, but with less conviction.

"You get back in that damned chair or I swear I'll blow his brains out!"

"Go ahead, stupid! He's going to die anyway if I don't

patch him up, so it makes damn all difference to me! And to cap it all you're going to fire a forty-five in a pressurized cabin at forty thousand feet. They teach you that at West Point, stupid?"

"*You watch your tongue!*"

"You watch it for me, Chewbacca! Now you get that first-aid kit or I swear to God I will fly you straight to Tel Aviv!"

His voice became a snarl. "OK, Captain Gallin, I'll get the first-aid kit and you can fix up your gentile boyfriend. But you have my word, as soon as we touch down in Montana, I am going to make you wish you were dead, and after that I will fulfill that wish."

"Yadda yadda yadda! Get the kit and save your breath." I heard the door close behind me and she sat back down in the pilot's seat. I heard her mutter, "You're going to need it." Then she looked at me. "I'm going to clean up the wound, then I'm going to give you something for the fever, OK?"

I nodded. "Promise me something."

"What?"

"I don't want to go wherever I am going, knowing I was responsible for your death."

"Shut up."

"I need you to promise me, when the time comes, you'll let me go and get to Nero."

"Yeah, whatever."

"Gallin, promise me."

"Listen, asshole. Wherever you're going, I'm going. Wherever I'm going, you're going. So shut up."

I groaned and closed my eyes. "You're going to Jewish

Heaven, to eat gefilte fish. I am going to atheist hell, to be prodded and poked by Jesuits with red-hot irons."

"Jesus! You're worse than I thought."

I went back into a deep, troubled sleep where judges in black robes were throwing red-hot coals at me in a Swedish sauna. I was vaguely aware of Gallin's hands, cool, slim and fresh, touching my arm and my face, pressing cool water onto my lips. At some point she gave me a tablet and made me swallow it. I sank back into blackness.

After a time that was timeless I opened my eyes. The cockpit was dark, illuminated only by the soft light from the controls. The only sound was the muted drone of the engines, and the gentle sound of breathing.

I sat a moment, looking out beyond the windshield, at infinity. Below us, and stretching out in front of us, was the blackness of the ocean, touched here and there by starlight. It blended seamlessly, invisibly, with the infinite, black ocean of space, peppered by stars.

My shoulder ached, but it was not the burning pain I had felt before. I turned my head and saw Gallin glance at me. She spoke quietly.

"It wasn't exactly a graze. It tore through the muscle and you'll have a great scar. But there was no serious damage."

"Thanks."

"You were in shock there for a while. How do you feel?"

"A bit groggy. How are we doing?"

With her eyes she indicated behind her. "On course for Montana."

I turned slowly and a little painfully. Colonel James Gordon was asleep in his chair with Gallin's Sig held loosely in his lap. He didn't have his seat belt on. I communicated that information to her by signs. She nodded, then said casually, "We should be sighting the coast soon, in an hour or so."

So that put us some six or seven hundred miles of the coast of New England. My mind was still sluggish and I wondered why she was telling me that. She glanced at me again and I knew she was trying to send me telepathic messages. To receive telepathic messages you need to have at the very least a brain, and I wasn't quite there yet. She closed her eyes and suppressed a sigh. She pointed with both fingers at the yoke and looked out at the blackness. I hunched my shoulders and apologized with my eyes. She sighed silently again and behind us Colonel James Gordon said, "What?"

Gallin looked back at him and echoed, "What?"

I thought I'd strike out for individuality and said, "Huh?"

Gordon said, "You said something."

Gallin rolled her eyes. "I said, 'How are you feeling?'"

He scowled. "Me?"

"No, dumbass. I don't give a damn how you're feeling. Mason woke up and I asked *him* how he was feeling."

"Oh..."

"Go take a leak and make us some coffee, will you. I'm falling asleep at the controls here."

"Screw you. I'm going to the can."

"I'll alert the media."

"Yah..." He muttered some obscenity, got to his feet and squeezed out through the cockpit door, closing it behind him. Gallin gave me an apologetic look, hunched her shoulders and said, "Sorry..."

The she leaned forward and pushed the yoke as far as it

would go forward. Next thing we were in a near vertical nosedive. The engines were screaming and the vast, black ocean was hurtling up to meet us. There was a kind of animal scream and a heavy body crashed against the door. I stared in horror at the altimeter. We were down to twenty thousand feet and dropping fast. "Gallin!" I said, "Pull up! *Pull up!*"

"Not yet!" She seemed to sieve the words through gritted teeth. "*Not yet!*"

Ten thousand feet, five thousand feet, and the engines seemed to be as terrified as I was. Two thousand feet, a thousand feet, "*Gallin! For Christ's sake pull up!*"

She pulled back on the yoke and we slowly started to level off. But ahead of us the ocean was still hurtling toward us, rising fast. At a hundred feet we became horizontal, with the ocean huge and swelling filling the windshield. Gordon's voice rose furious and bellowing beyond the door. Gallin ignored him and heaved on the yoke again, but this time pulling it toward her. "Now, you son of a bitch!"

The nose pulled up and suddenly we were hurtling in a steep climb toward the stars. I felt myself crushed into the seat and heard a blood-curdling scream from behind me as gravity tried to drag the colonel through the tail of the plane, down toward the Atlantic.

When we had reached thirty thousand feet, she grinned at me. "What do you think? One more time for the sake of completeness?"

"You're actually enjoying this, aren't you?"

She gave a short chortle and thrust the yoke forward again. There was no scream this time, just a sickening thud as the colonel hit the cockpit wall. At a thousand feet she pulled up again and started a gentle climb. She undid her harness and said, "You have the conn, Mr. Spock." She got to her feet and at the door she paused. "I'll be back."

"I hope you didn't kill him, Gallin. We need that guy alive."

She disappeared and returned a few moments later.

"He's not dead, but do you know how hard it is to find rope on a medium-sized private luxury jet?"

"That's probably a problem most people don't encounter in life, Gallin."

"Right?"

"So what did you do?

"I had two bootlaces left. I also pulled off his pants and tied his wrists with them."

I frowned at her. "Will they hold?"

"I don't think so. But he's in pretty bad shape. I don't think he's going to cause us much trouble. Besides, I recovered this." She held up her P226.

I nodded. My brain still felt numb and my shoulder was starting to ache again. "We need to decide what we're going to do. We need to get in touch with Nero somehow. Or at least find out what's happened to him."

She leaned her backside against the pilot's seat. "Find out how? Anyone we might ask is suspect."

"What about your father?"

She shook her head. "I can ask again, but he already told us, all he knows is that Nero went off the air."

"So we have to go to the last place we know he was going."

"Groom Lake." I nodded. She sighed. "You get shot for just looking at that place. We come in with a plane on an unauthorized flight trajectory, we don't stand a chance."

She stared out at the black night ahead of us. I said, "So we do a Roswell."

"We do a what, Mr. Gray?"

"We do a Roswell. We are probably cleared for Montana. So when we get there we turn south and drop real low, below radar. We just need to cross Idaho and part of Nevada. That's what, six hundred miles? An hour, and let's face it, it's practically all remote desert. We just have to stay off the radar. Out there that won't be hard. When we are closing in on Groom Lake, round about Rachel, we come down in the desert and finish the route on foot."

She was gazing at me like I'd just climbed out of a Petri dish. "Your plan is to cross two states at below five hundred feet and then crash in the desert? That's your plan?"

"Yeah."

"That's his plan."

"You work with what you've got, right?"

"Mom, I died, because I went with a man who thought crashing a plane was a plan."

"OK, it's a bad plan. Improve it."

"No, crossing the Antarctic with insufficient clothes and food is a bad plan. This, crashing a plane in the Nevada desert, is something you do on YouTube to entertain psychotic rednecks."

"OK, so we film it on our cell phones and post it on YouTube. We'll be famous. Gallin, what other options do we have? We land in the desert and we go in on foot, waving a white flag, and hope to Christ Nero is there." She shook her head, still gazing out at the blackness. I went on. "Let's face it. The fact that the strike hasn't happened yet suggests he is still alive and operative."

She studied my face a moment. "At Groom Lake?"

"That's the best information we have."

"OK, Mason, but if I die you'll have to answer to my mother."

"Hey, where you go, I go, remember?"

"You're not going to atheist hell anymore?"

"If I am, I'm taking you with me."

She went and made some chicken soup which, though I had long since ceased to have a kid's soul, helped. We flew on in silence, trailing the pre-dawn behind us. She slept for a couple of hours and, as we crossed the state line between South Dakota and Montana, she opened her eyes and squinted at the graying sky.

"Billings?"

"How would you know that?"

"I told my unconscious to tell me when we got to Billings."

"That would explain it. You want to give me the heading for Groom Lake? I'm dropping to five hundred feet, or a stupidly low height over Yellowstone Park."

"You OK?"

"Might be an idea if you drank a gallon of coffee and took the controls for an hour. I'll land it if you like."

"Oh, you figure after a rest you'll be OK to crash it?"

"I think so."

She grinned, leaned over and pinched my cheek, which was disturbing. "Ayy!" she said, "I'll miss you when you're gone."

She drank a gallon of coffee and I tried to sleep for an

hour. Before we had been flying east to west, with the rising sun on our tail. Now, on a southwesterly bearing, the sun began to rise, blood-red and burnished gold on our portside. The few times I opened my eyes it blinded me, and as I looked away I saw mountain peaks and endless forests racing past just a couple of hundred feet below us, dropping suddenly into deep valleys, ravines and canyons.

Then my eyes would grow heavy again and I would sink into troubled dreams about my car, my house in DC and my cat, Manny Pacquiao. They were all being repossessed by Nero, who occupied a gigantic black hole at the center of the galaxy. "Gravity pulls everything in," he was saying, "Gravity pulls everything down..."

I opened my eyes and there was a breakfast sun shining through the port window. All around us there was dry, red and ochre desert, sculpted by cruel winds.

"Welcome to hell," Gallin said, and smiled at me. "We are going down. Brace."

I just had time to say, "Jesus! Buy a guy a drink!" before the world was filled with the screaming of airbrakes and the insane hurtling of huge red and ochre objects leaping toward the windshield. Next thing there was only dust, swirling, surging, thick like dirty smoke. It took only a second or two. Then I realized if I could see these things I had not braced. Then there was a violent smash that jarred every bone in my body. The noise filled the whole world with twisted, agonizing metal screams. For a millisecond we were suspended in timeless silence and space. Then we pounded the earth again. I whiplashed forward and the air was kicked out of my lungs. Rocks and sand loomed in the windshield. I felt a strange weightlessness and realized the jet was trying to do a headstand. Somebody was screaming in my head. The forward momentum lifted us in the air and we belly-flopped again. I felt every vertebra in my body crushed. Then we slewed sideways and came to a stop in a world of dust and pain.

I sat for a while, groaning and swearing. Gallin's voice saying, "I told you to brace," didn't help.

"*You couldn't have warned me?*" I shouted, not just at Gallin but at the universe as a whole about life in general.

"Quit griping. I spent five minutes calling you. All you could say was, 'Please don't take my cat.'"

I ignored her and gingerly undid my harness. "You know I'm wounded, right?"

"I know you're a big girl's blouse. It was a flesh wound."

I stood. It wasn't easy. Outside the world was a Martian landscape of lingering red mist. "We need to check on the colonel. That landing probably killed him. I told you to let me do it."

"Asleep? Worrying about your cat? Sure." I reached for the cockpit door and pulled it open. Behind me she was saying, "Besides, you think I never crashed a plane before?"

"I'm sure you have." The cabin was a forest of blue tubes and yellow oxygen masks dangling like lianas over the seats. There was remarkably little damage, except that the door had been busted open and was lying mangled out in the desert. "Where did you say the colonel was?"

"Right there." She appeared at my shoulder and pointed at the nearest table set in front of a leather armchair. "I put him between the chair and the table to immobilize him as much as possible."

"Yeah? Well, he seems to have been mobilized since then.

Either he's been thrown free in a freak of dynamics, or he has slipped his bonds and made an escape."

"Jesus, what is this guy made of?"

I didn't know what to say. "People as close to death as we are, Gallin, should not take the Lord's name in vain. Whatever he's made of, we need to find him, and fast."

SIXTEEN

Nero ran his fingers through his thinning hair and emitted a laborious grunt. He had been long hours without a proper meal and his humor was becoming dangerously prickly. So far the missiles had not been launched from the satellite. Though that had given them time, the fact remained that the launch could still come at any moment. The attack was still very much on, and the satellite was sitting there, invisible in the blue sky, watching them and waiting for they knew not what. Was Putin having a crisis of conscience? Had there been a palace coup in Russia? Was there some other, unknown reason why they had not yet struck? There was no way of knowing. The White House was as silent as the tomb, the Pentagon was in crisis trying to find out what the hell was going on, and the Kremlin was refusing to talk to anyone.

The best bet was that when they had failed to recapture Rusenko they had reset the launch codes and the time of launch, confident the Pentagon would not have time to stop it. And this time there would be no failure. They would have everything tied down and secured, and they would rain devastation down upon the Western world.

Nero had not been idle. He had spent the last several hours attempting to lure the satellite into moving. He had threatened it with missiles, he had brought other satellites into closer proximity and had even peppered a quadrant of the sky with laser fire, hoping to provoke the satellite into firing its boosters. But it had remained immobile and invisible. If they had got hold of Rusenko earlier, when they were supposed to, if they had not been betrayed, they would have been able to pinpoint the satellite and take it out. But with the Russians alerted to his defection, they had managed to move the satellite and effectively hide it. That had at least bought them some time, but Nero needed more than time. He needed to find the damned satellite and destroy it!

And as if the situation were not stressful enough, he was probably now guilty of treason, he had taken control of a top-secret military research facility and he was engaged in what amounted to an act of war against Russia.

If all of this resulted in the destruction of the satellite, well and good. But as it stood, there was absolutely no guarantee of that; and to complicate matters further, as far as he was aware, the president had gone into hiding in Montana. The country didn't know it, but they were effectively facing nuclear devastation rudderless and without a captain at the helm.

Brigadier General Bill Clancy leaned across the highly polished table in the darkened room, illuminated only by the computer monitors. His voice was edged by growing despair.

"Nero, we have to do something."

Nero's voice was dead, almost a whisper. "What can we do? The damned thing is invisible and it does not respond to provocation."

The brigadier general turned on Rusenko. "Dr. Rusenko! For God's sake! There must be something you can do! Hack into its onboard computers! There must be something you know about this damned satellite that we can use!"

He shook his head and ran his fingers through his thin hair. "Two things will make the satellite give away its position, and then only for a second. If it engages its thrusters in order to maneuver, or if it fires its lasers to defend itself from a missile. But in order to fire a missile at it, we need to know where it is!"

"It will slip behind the horizon soon." It was Dr. Patel.

Suddenly Nero slammed his fat palm down on the table. They all turned to stare at him. There was a kind of madness in his eyes.

"Gentlemen," he said, "if we are to face nuclear annihilation, then let us at least take first blood! We shall strike first!"

He surveyed the faces, the collective expression of horror, and then the double horror as it dawned on them that what he had said actually made some horrific kind of sense. When madness is the norm, then madness makes sense.

"Let me tell you," he boomed, "what we are going to do!"

But he was brought up short by frantic shouts from below, and boots tramping on the iron staircase. A breathless voice shouted for the general.

"General Clancy, sir! Sir! Incoming!" it shouted.

They all stood. Nero felt the blood drain from his face. His heart pounded. He heard himself mutter, "What is he saying?"

The breathless soldier appeared at the top of the stairs, pointing south and east. "Coming in low over the desert, sir. We thought first it was a missile, sir. But it's too big. Looks like a jet crash-landing!"

The brigadier general turned to stare at Nero. They exchanged silent thoughts. The brigadier turned back to his man. "Send a team. If there are survivors, bring them in!"

———

WE WERE in what seemed to be a dry riverbed. I am more of an urban warrior, but Gallin had experience of desert operations and pretty soon found the colonel's tracks. At first they followed the slight incline uphill, but after ten or fifteen paces he turned sharply west, toward a large hill with an outcrop of rocks on top, less than half a mile away.

I frowned at Gallin in the copper glow of the rising sun. "He's not armed, right?"

"Not unless he starts throwing rocks at us." I gave her a look that said she wasn't convincing me much. She jerked her head toward the rocks. "C'mon, big guy. He can't have got far, and he is badly banged up. He's probably lying face-down in the sand unconscious."

She set off, pushing through the sand, and I went after her. "Did you ever see *The Terminator*?"

"Of course. Great movie."

"I have this feeling we are going to find him, he's going

to sit up suddenly with no expression on his face and stab us in the eye with his finger."

"Are you still delirious, Mason?"

I didn't answer. I was busy trying to work out whether I had more pain or more body. I decided there was definitely more pain than body.

"So where are we in relation to the base?"

She pointed. "About eight or ten miles northeast. Basically, follow the dry riverbed."

"Eight or ten miles. In this desert, those two miles can be the difference between life and death."

"I didn't know you could be such a prima donna. I thought you were tough and resourceful. Don't you ever train in the desert? Ten miles, two miles an hour, five hours. Stick to the shade. When you pee, you collect up the saturated earth, you make a structure of sticks around it and lay plastic over the structure, like a greenhouse, with a small cup underneath. Then you let the sun evaporate the pure water from your urine, it condenses on the plastic and drips into your cup."

"I'm more of a Chateau Margot 1982 kind of guy."

"You never did survival training?"

We were approaching a low sand dune. She gestured me to keep talking, but we should separate to approach from the angles. I started to move right.

"For me," I continued, "I was more into the urban aspect. How to tail someone in the city, how to arrange a dead drop successfully, the correct way to order a martini..."

We both had our weapons out by then, held out in front of us. We crested the dune and found Colonel James Gordon forty paces farther on, lying facedown in the sand. I ran, thrusting my weapon in my belt as I went, while Gallin followed a little behind, covering me.

I hunkered down beside him and pulled his face out of the sand. He was still alive, but badly bruised. I checked his pulse. It was steady but slow.

"OK, Tonto," I said, "we caught him, now what do we do with him? I have to tell you that five hours of walking through the desert at a hundred degrees in the shade, dragging King Kong along and drinking my own pee, does not appeal to me much."

"Don't worry about it, J. Lo. We're going to have about fifty grunts and a lieutenant to help us in just about five minutes. This is Area 51, Mason. They have cameras watching the cameras in this place. They saw us come down and they are on their way"

I nodded. "I guess so."

She wasn't wrong. She stayed with the prone colonel and I walked the short distance to the top of the dune. A distant plume of dust soon revealed two trucks barreling toward us from the direction of the base. I raised my arms and waved them in the air. The first truck drove past, making for the downed Bombardier, but the second came to a halt at the base of the dune. While a dozen soldiers sprang from the rear, a lieutenant swung down from the cab pulling a Glock from his holster.

"*Keep your hands in the air!*" he bellowed. "*This is a restricted area! What are you doing here?*"

He and his men were marching up the sand dune, training their weapons on me as he shouted.

I kept my hands in the air but looked over at where the

first truck was pulling up beside the crashed jet. I looked back at him where he was struggling up the hill.

"Seriously? What are we doing here? Our jet crashed. That's why your pal went to the, uh, crashed jet."

Most of my irony was wasted on him. Because when he got to the top of the dune he saw Gallin and the colonel and he waved his weapon at them and shouted. "On your feet! Put your hands in the air!"

"Lieutenant," I said it mildly. "Son, you need to relax and take in what is going on here. That man is US Army Colonel James Gordon, military attaché at the American Embassy in Madrid. The woman beside him is Captain Aila Gallin, of the Mossad, currently seconded to the Office of the Director of Intelligence Networks, and I am Captain Alex Mason, of that same organization. That man is our prisoner and we are here to see the base commander, and, if he is here, the director of ODIN."

He stared at me for a long moment, then turned to his sergeant.

"All right, load them in the back of the truck. Take them to Hangar Twelve."

They took our weapons and escorted us down the dune, where we were assisted into the back of the truck. Colonel Gordon wasn't so much escorted as carried and dumped. The soldiers climbed in with us and sat on the benches looking insolently blank, the way only soldiers know how. One or two of them eyed the colonel where he lay. I leaned forward and asked the nearest one—a big bald guy with lots of tattoos—"Hey, is it true what they say? I often wondered. Is there a UFO here? And bodies?"

He smiled and shook his head. "No, of course not. With

all the attention this place gets, they shipped them out to Minot Air Force Base, in North Dakota."

"Right..."

After a moment they all laughed. It was a strained laugh, but I joined in.

———

NERO GLARED at me across the table with outraged eyes. His bottom lip twitched for a while.

"I assumed you were dead!" he said.

"I'll try harder next time, sir."

"You're being facetious." It was almost a question. "I suppose you haven't eaten." I frowned, trying to remember. "You see!" he said, and gestured at me with an open hand. "For goodness sake, somebody find something edible—and a bottle of wine!"

"Irish," I said, "Bushmills?" I pointed at my shoulder like it was an explanation. "I was shot."

Feet scurried and Nero's scowl deepened. "Are you crippled? Incapacitated?"

I shook my head. "No."

He turned his attention to Gallin. "You?"

"Am I crippled or incapacitated?" He nodded. She shook her head. "Nah."

He grunted. I pointed at my cell and Gallin's on the table. "Statements from Gordon and Romano. I tried to call you..."

"The decision was taken to come here. It was necessary to go off the air. I trusted if you were alive you would have the intelligence to come here. Though as I say, I assumed you were dead."

A couple of hamburgers and a bottle of wine appeared in front of me, with a couple of glasses. That was all followed by a bottle of Bushmills and a couple of tumblers. I watched Nero's lip curl.

"A hamburger..." he said. "Well, needs must when the devil drives."

I drained the glass of wine, refilled and bit into the burger. Gallin too was eating hungrily beside me. Nero watched us a moment, then started to speak.

"We have not as yet been able to locate the satellite. We are about to make what might be our final attempt. Meanwhile, the president has apparently disappeared in Montana. He has a ranch up there which he has constructed for himself, and whether he has sought refuge there, or whether he is a prisoner there, we have no idea. The White House has gone silent, as has the Pentagon. Nobody knows what anybody else is doing, and the one linchpin which should be holding everything together has vanished."

I frowned and spoke with my mouth full. "Can't you send someone to fetch him?"

"Who? Whom can I trust? When even General Pat O'Connor seems to be a Russian agent! The military attaché at the embassy in Madrid is a traitor! Nobody knows whom to follow because nobody knows what side is the right side!"

I finished the burger, shaking my head, drained my glass and poured myself a medicinal shot of Bushmills, still shaking my head. The alcohol was soothing and I really needed to sleep and rest.

"There must be somebody you can trust, sir, to fly up there, drop in and see what's going on. I mean, he must have staff up there..."

I trailed off with my whiskey halfway to my mouth, aware that Nero was staring at me with absolutely no expression. I turned and looked at Gallin. She had her jaw slightly open, staring at Nero, with a small piece of burger in her hand.

She suddenly gave a heavy sigh. "You'd better pour me a shot of that whiskey," she said. "I am going to need it."

I looked back at Nero, frowning, incredulous. "You want *me* to go to Montana, sir?"

I tried to inject as much pain and pathos into the question as I could, but he didn't seem to notice.

"We need to know what has happened to the president. There is no other way."

I pointed to the cell phones. "According to Gordon and Romano..."

"Whatever Gordon and Romano may have alleged," he cut me short, "the office of president of the United States is a sacred office which *cannot* betray the people of America. It is therefore essential that my most trusted agent should go and rescue the person of the president, if he should need rescuing."

Gallin scowled. "What about me? He won't make it without me!"

"They are fueling a jet as we speak. Go and speak to the sergeant about what equipment you'll need. Have your shoulder dressed, painkillers, all that. Change into something more suitable, and report to me as soon as you know something."

"Will you answer the phone this time, sir?" I asked sourly.

He flicked his fingers at me. "Go!"

SEVENTEEN

WE WERE FLYING LOW OVER UTAH IN A SMALL JET doing better than seven hundred miles per hour, and checking our hastily assembled kit. We had two large rucksacks with their contents strewn on the floor. They consisted of two Heckler & Koch 416 assault rifles with AG-HK416 grenade launchers and infrared telescopic sights. We had two Sig Sauer P226 with extended magazines plus two suppressed Maxim 9s. I had also found and taken possession of one hickory takedown bow with twelve carbon arrows with razor-sharp broadheads. Because, however well you suppress a firearm, it still makes a noise, but a good bow will just whisper death in your ear.

They'd had no commando fighting knives, so we'd taken a couple of Bowie knives instead. In addition, we had selected two sets of night-vision goggles, two pairs of binoculars, six cakes of C4 each, with remote detonators and enough ammunition to fuel a South American revolution.

I took a Sig, shoved in a magazine and slipped it behind

my back in my waistband and holstered a Maxim 9 at my hip. Then I shoved the knife into my boot. Everything else would stay in the bags till we were on the ground.

It was nearing five o'clock, and sunset was a good three hours away. The gray desert below was turning to copper and the shadows of what few trees there were, were stretching long across the arid hills.

From the cockpit the pilot said, "Fifteen minutes."

We pulled on our parachutes and snapped the harnesses. I glanced at Gallin and grunted. "I'd hoped at least for the cover of dark."

She shrugged. "Swings and roundabouts. They can see us, but we also get a chance to see what we're getting into."

I thought about it a moment. "Yeah," I said at last. "Because we really have zero idea what is waiting for us there. This is crazy."

She gave a single nod and we held each other's eye. "Golden rule," she said. "Prepare, prepare, prepare. But we're going in blind."

She sighed. "I haven't smoked for a few years. I'm not about to start again. But if I did, this would be the time."

"Yeah, thanks. Bit of positive thinking. Any other last wishes?"

She grinned. "Yes, but I am not going to tell you until we are literally seconds from death."

"Nice."

"Five minutes! Positions please."

A moment later the door hissed open, we approached and peered out. We were about five hundred feet up and speeding over rugged, forested mountain terrain. We pulled on our helmets and heard the pilot's voice in our ears.

"Coming up on Missoula on the right-hand side. Target is four minutes and counting."

We braced ourselves. I would go first. She would follow. A five-hundred-foot drop was fast, and we would be dropping into woodland. Then it would be a matter of collecting up the chutes, concealing them and heading straight for the ranch.

"One minute and counting..."

We had passed Missoula and were banking west over a shallow, fertile valley. I saw a road, a cluster of houses, and then we were over forest again. I saw a large, sprawling ranch in the distance and a clearing a few hundred yards away. The pilot's voice snapped, "Go one!" and I hurled myself out of the plane.

I was in midair. It was freezing cold. For a moment all I could see was the empty sky above me. Gallin floated into view with her hands and legs spread-eagled and I yanked at the ripcord. I felt the jolt and then we were sailing slowly in the late, cold sunshine toward a clearing in the trees half a mile from the ranch.

We hit the ground, rolled and within less than a minute we had gathered up the parachutes and concealed them buried in a shallow grave beneath dense ferns. Then we set off at a steady trot through the woods toward the ranch, with absolutely no idea what we were going to encounter there.

We climbed steadily for five minutes in a roughly northerly direction, with the forest and the undergrowth of ferns and bushes growing thicker as we went. Pretty soon we had to slow to a walk, and when we finally came to the crest of the hill we dropped and lay on our bellies, peering through the leaves at the shallow valley ahead of us.

Gallin said, "So here's the bit we haven't planned for. This is a secure area, a presidential residence. In theory, the president is just chilling here while he contemplates affairs of state. We encounter armed guards. What do we do?"

I nodded. "OK, here's how we deal with it. If we run across a patrol and they stop us, we make like lost ramblers and ask for directions to Evaro. As soon as their backs are turned we take 'em down and interrogate them. Where is the president and why is he incommunicado?"

"I like it. It's elegant."

We set off again. It was still two hours till sunset, but because of the mountains the sun was behind the ridges and the trees, and darkness started closing in early. That at least to me was a relief.

We came to a road that crossed our path. Fifty yards to my right I saw a fork and a sign that pointed to Charity Peak. We crossed the road at a run and scrambled into the forest again. Here it became more dense, and the slope was steeper. We had to struggle to climb, pulling ourselves by gripping at the trees and the branches. After another five minutes we crested the hill and began to scramble down a steep, densely wooded slope. Now the struggle was to keep from sliding down.

Then we suddenly found ourselves stumbling onto blacktop. We were still in deep forest, but we were on a straight stretch of road beneath towering trees. There was forest behind us, ahead of us and on either side. And on my left, just ten paces away, there was a Dodge RAM.

Leaning against it was a man in camouflage with a butt

in his mouth. He had a holstered sidearm at his hip, and an M16 hanging on his shoulder. He was watching us. Nice and slow he thumped the side of the truck, then pushed himself off and started strolling toward us. Behind him a second guy climbed out, but through the rear window I could make out two heads. Obviously they didn't figure we warranted all four of them.

The guy approaching us took a final drag of his cigarette, examined the glowing tip like he might have left something behind, and dropped the butt on the ground, where he trod on it.

I had a slow burn in my gut. The uniform looked real enough and so did the M16, but to the best of my knowledge the United States Army does not use twenty-year-old Dodge RAMs. I glanced at Gallin. She slipped off her rucksack and dumped it on the ground like she was tired, and I saw the fingers of her right hand loosen the flap where her assault rifle was while she watched the soldier approach.

I put a smile on my face. Behind him the passenger door opened and a taller, bigger guy with no hair and dark olive skin climbed out too. His sidearm was holstered, but the holster was unclipped and he had an assault rifle in his hand. He approached watching us with a face that had grown accustomed to scowling.

The guy who'd been smoking said, "Howdy, y'all. Where y'all headed?"

For a moment I thought he was joking, then realized he actually spoke like that. I broadened my smile and said, "Good evening, we were looking for Charity Peak, but we seem to have got lost."

He regarded me for a long moment with unfriendly eyes.

"There is a trail," he said, "that'll take you all the way. Bit late to be goin' up there now, friend. Be night time by the time you git there, and mighty cold. My advice to you would be to head on back home."

His big pal had come up behind him. He regarded Gallin a second with no expression, then jerked his chin at me. He had a voice like a tectonic disturbance. "You're out at this time of the evening trying to get to Charity Peak? That's bullshit, man."

I grimaced. "Well, as I say, we started a lot earlier. We decided to go cross country... Can you advise us how to get back on the right track for the peak?"

The smoker looked at his pal and grinned. He spoke to me without looking at me, "You got money? How much money you got?"

I made a face of confusion and frowned at Gallin. She had arched a dangerous eyebrow. "Money? I don't know, a hundred bucks? Why?"

But his pal's eyes were already traveling to our backpacks and he was frowning. "What you got in the sacks there?"

"These?" I said.

The smoker said, "Yeah, those. Tell you what, pal. Let's take you over to the trees there by the truck. I think we are going to conduct ourselves a strip search."

I put my hands up. "Oh, no, now look. You don't need to do that. We don't want any trouble. We'll just be on our way..."

They both pulled their sidearms and pointed them at me. The smoker smiled. "You ain't gonna git no trouble, boy, if you do like you're told. Now you just bring your stuff over to the truck there. We have a little look at your kit," he laughed, "and then we'll have a look at the lady's kit." He laughed and they ushered as across the road and into the undergrowth beside the truck. I was talking quietly to Gallin all the while.

"Don't worry, honey. These are United States soldiers. They're probably just a little high-spirited. I'm sure it'll be OK."

She watched me with frightened eyes while I spoke.

"They're not going to do anything to me, are they, darling? Why are they pointing guns at us?"

We had come to a halt. I tried to adopt the kind of voice my schoolteachers used to try and make me see reason. I started as they usually started, with, "Now look here, you boys must be attached to a regiment..."

The smoker looked at me and said, "Shut up." To Gallin he said, "Take your clothes off, sweet cheeks."

I said, "You must be out of your mind! You can't do this!"

He thrust his Glock in my face and snarled, "Can it! Keep talking and—"

He didn't get any further. I leaned to the left, smashed my right palm into his wrist and grabbed the barrel of the Glock with my left, levering it savagely in toward his face. I didn't want any gunfire—not yet, anyway—so I kicked him hard in the groin and as my foot came down I smashed my elbow into his jaw. He fell with a heavy thud. The big guy was frowning uncomprehendingly at Gallin's Sig, which was pointing at his chest. I held out my hand and he gave me his M16.

"What is this," I asked him, "a new recreational activity

for the Secret Service? To rob and rape hikers in the Montana wilderness?"

He narrowed his eyes at me. "Screw you."

"Hey! I'm asking you a question, stupid! I'm Captain Alex Mason of the Office of the Director of Intelligence Networks, and this is Captain Aila Gallin. Now unless you're keen to spend the next twenty years in a state penitentiary, you'd better start talking."

"I was talking," he said, and grinned an ugly grin. "I said screw you. We the Presidential Palace Guard, see? I don't gotta tell you nothin'."

Gallin looked at me with narrowed eyes. "*The Presidential Palace Guard?* What the hell is that? Who is your commanding officer?"

"General Pat O'Connor and the president. Nobody tells us what to do, 'cept the general and the president."

I was shaking my head in growing disbelief. "Where were you recruited, soldier?"

He looked defiant. "Mexico."

"You were recruited from a private security company, weren't you?"

"So what?"

"Jesus, Christ!" I turned to Gallin. "That son of a bitch has recruited a private army and he has the president under house arrest, telling him it's for his own safety!" I turned back to the hulk. "How many of you are there?"

The answer came from behind me. "Too many for you, Captain Mason. Game over."

I turned. There were two of them and they both had automatic rifles. One had the same unevolved look as the guy we'd been speaking to. The other bore a lieutenant's insignia on his sleeve. He was in his thirties and had that crazy, intense stare that fanatics sometimes get. I smiled on the ironic side of my face.

"But *you're* not private security, are you?"

"Drop your weapon, Mason. You too, sweet cheeks."

I looked at Gallin and sighed. "I really didn't want to have to do this."

She shrugged. "What can you do?"

It was pretty spectacular. She gave a little hop. It's called a pendulum. You make a small jump, take a long, sideways step with your right foot and as your left foot catches up you lash out in a side kick with your right foot. It's a devastating kick that carries a huge amount of kinetic energy.

Gallin executed it exquisitely, and smashed her heel square into the gorilla's windpipe. As she came down she smashed the butt of her Sig into his temple and he was dead by the time he hit the ground. It took less than a second and she was standing behind the lieutenant with her Sig pointed at the back of her neck.

The first gorilla was having trouble keeping up with the fluid situation and lunged at me with both hands, reaching for his M16. I let him have it, and as he snatched it I pulled the Maxim and put two rounds into his head. While I was at it I put the smoker out of his misery too. Then I turned to the lieutenant.

"You were saying?"

He shook his head. "You have no idea."

I grabbed him by his collar and dragged him deeper into the woods with Gallin covering him from behind. After thirty yards or so I kicked him in the back of the knee and threw him on the ground.

"OK, Lieutenant. We can do this one of two ways. And I have to tell you we do not have much time to waste. So, I am going to start blowing off your joints. I'll start with your wrists and your ankles, then your elbows and your knees…"

"Stop, stop, stop!"

"What I don't want to have to do, Lieutenant, is have to prove to you that I mean business. We just don't have the time."

Gallin cut in. "How many men in this Presidential Guard?"

"One hundred so far, but it is due to expand."

"Where are they located?"

"They are all at the ranch, guarding the president."

"Guarding him against *what?*"

He shook his head. "You don't know. You don't realize."

I snarled. "That's why we're asking you, genius! One more stupid comment like that and I blow your right knee off. Guarding the president against *what?*"

"There is a coup in progress at the Pentagon. They are going to declare a state of martial law. The FEMA camps are already set up and operational all over the damn country. I've seen them. There are eight thousand of them, man, everywhere."

"Who recruited you?"

"The general."

"What general?"

"General Pat O'Connor. He works directly with the president. I have seen them together and I have spoken with the president. I know this is real, man!"

"What about the others? How were they recruited?"

"A few of us are Army, chosen personally by General

O'Connor. But most are private sector, from Eastern Europe and South America."

"Mercenaries."

"Yeah."

I stared at Gallin. "This, this right here is how these things go wrong." I looked down at the lieutenant. "And who is supposed to be leading this coup, Lieutenant?"

"The Russians, with the help of the Chinese. They have a satellite..."

"Dumbass."

I pulled his laces, tied his ankles and his wrists and stuffed his socks in his mouth.

Gallin watched me do it. "We just going to leave him here?"

"What else can we do?"

She shook her head. "This is a mess. There are a hundred men down there."

"Ninety-six."

"And the president convinced he is being protected by General O'Connor! How can this happen? What about all his other advisers? Didn't they see this coming?"

I asked, "How far are we from the ranch?"

"Less than a mile. These guys will check in regularly. When they don't they'll go red alert and come looking for them."

"So while they're looking for us out here, we'll be looking for the president in there." I hesitated while she searched my face. "You want out?" I asked.

"Don't be stupid," she said. "Come on, we'll be there in half an hour."

EIGHTEEN

AT SHORTLY BEFORE EIGHT, AS THE SUN WAS setting behind the mountains in the west, the cold dark seemed to enfold us. We lay on our bellies, side by side, shuddering slightly as we watched the lights come on in the presidential ranch below.

Gallin shook her head. "I can't believe we're doing this. It's like breaking in to Camp David to kidnap the president. Can you imagine the security they have down there?"

I nodded. "It will be sophisticated, but not as much as you might think."

She frowned at me. "Explain."

"OK, it seems pretty clear that Boris Semenov, Peter Romano, O'Connor and Gordon dreamed up this plan with the cooperation of a bunch of lunatics back in Moscow."

"So?"

"Give me a chance. Now O'Connor's job was clearly to get close to the president, persuade him that the USA was at serious risk from Russia, and that he should build himself a ranch out here in Montana where he could retreat in case of a Russian attack."

"OK, that makes sense."

"Meantime, O'Connor is recruiting a small army of mercenaries and psychopaths to keep the place secure. He is going to install some high-tech security, for sure, but not the kind of stuff you'll see at the White House or Camp David."

"Why not?"

"First because it's too expensive and not necessary." I smiled at her. "After all, the bad guys are already on the inside. Second, he wants to keep it low key. To everybody else this is just the president building himself a ranch in Montana. He doesn't want to alert people that he's building a fortress." I shrugged. "And besides, as far as they are concerned, in a few hours we are going to be looking at Armageddon. That ranch is going to be a bunker with a hundred armed men, and video surveillance. Not a lot more."

She looked skeptical. "You're awful sure of yourself."

I put the binoculars to my eyes and stared down at the building.

It was set in a wide clearing with thick forest on all sides. A narrow, winding track through the woods connected it to the outside world. Focusing in on the building I saw that as well as having the protection of the trees, the clearing was surrounded by a high-perimeter fence that consisted of a steel frame covered in wire mesh. I spoke quietly, "Two gets you twenty that fence is electrified, though."

"No doubt. And it will not only fry you, it will set off an alarm, too."

I grunted. Inside that outer, perimeter fence there was a space of about seven feet which was laid with rolls of barbed wire, and after that there was a wall, eight feet high and made of solid concrete.

Gallin grunted. "It's not a ranch, it's a goddamn fortress."

Within the wall there were several buildings. At the center was a large, three-storey Spanish villa, with red corrugated tile roofs and a large veranda. At about a hundred and fifty feet from the house were the steel gates that gave access to the compound. One gate in the wall, the other in the barbed-wire fence.

Behind the house there was a large walled garden with a maze, a swimming pool and a tennis court. Anyone inside the house or that garden would be shut off from the rest of the ranch, invisible from it, and unable to see it. Presumably that was where they kept the president.

The rest of the compound, invisible from the house, was taken up with a small barracks and a parking area for four trucks, a couple of Hummers, four Land Rovers and a small fleet of Jeeps.

I counted what soldiers I could see. They were discretely positioned around the house, on the roof and the veranda, and around the perimeter of the garden. I saw twenty. I wondered where the other seventy-six were.

Dusk was suddenly turning to night and in an instant the entire place was floodlit with powerful lights, bright as day.

I pulled the cell Nero had given me from my pocket and called him. When he answered he sounded strained.

"Tell me."

"I have good news and I have bad news. The good news is that the president has been kidnapped and is being held by General O'Connor and a force of one hundred mercenaries at his Evaro Ranch, which is in fact nothing less than a fortress."

"That is the good news, Alex? Your capacity for face-tiousness never ceases to amaze me. So what is the bad news, then?"

"He doesn't know it. He thinks he is being protected from a Russian invasion and that General O'Connor is his only ally. Sir, you need to open a line of communication with the Pentagon and tell them what is going on."

"We are trying, Alex, but O'Connor has done the same thing. It is like an insane Mexican standoff and neither the White House nor the Pentagon knows whom to believe."

"We can't take this facility alone, sir. Even a handful of Marines, some Delta operators..."

"I'll see what I can do, Alex, but you must understand, we have no time. We are minutes away from a strike..."

"Yes sir, I understand." I hung up. "We're on our own. So how are we going to do this?"

She was watching the place through her binoculars. "That guy at the front of the house..." I looked. "That's O'Connor. He's talking to an officer. I can't make out his rank."

I said, "He's giving him the bad news. The patrol didn't check in."

He was spreading his hands and shrugging his shoulders, like he was making excuses. Meanwhile O'Connor was waving his hands and shouting. In a sudden rush of fury O'Connor slapped and kicked the officer, who cowered. He then shouted something, pointing at the gate, and the officer ran away, apparently gesticulating and shouting.

Within a couple of minutes a large group of men in fatigues had mustered in front of the house, along with two Land Rovers and four Jeeps. The general was addressing them personally, and by his movements he wasn't telling them how smart they looked.

"I'm counting fifty men," she muttered. "That's twenty-four in the vehicles, what are the other twenty-six going to do?"

The answer came pretty soon. The two gates opened and the six vehicles roared out along the long, winding road, through the forest. Their mission was clear: to find the missing patrol and establish what had happened to them. It would be only a matter of time before they found the lieutenant and he told them.

Meanwhile, the remaining twenty-six foot soldiers streamed out after the vehicles at a steady run and divided into three six-man teams and one seven-man team. One headed north, one east and one west, and the fourth headed straight for us.

I muttered something obscene under my breath. "These are mercenaries, Gallin. They are experienced and professional. This is going to cost us time we can't afford, and sooner or later they will find us."

I was surprised to see she was smiling.

"Relax, we have the advantage here. It's dark and we have night-vision goggles. Jungle warfare, like desert warfare, is all about staying hidden and using the element of surprise. Right now we know where they are, but they don't even know for sure if we're here at all. So we are going to use knives, the bow and the Maxim 9s."

I nodded. "OK." I watched the patrol moving out of the glow of the camp and into the growing darkness, trudging across the open ground. I spoke half to myself. "OK, we'll leave them small tracks and clues to follow. Let them think we are trying to escape. They'll follow, we'll wait for them."

She nodded. "That's how it's done."

I dropped my voice, speaking quietly in the growing dark. "We have to maximize this opportunity. This is like Crecy and Poitiers, right? If we get this right we can take out a quarter of their men before they realize what has happened."

"They will be in radio contact with each other."

"But they'll also be trying to observe radio silence. Every conversation and each crackle gives us a location."

"OK."

"We want to take out all four teams, then we move in on the ranch."

She gave me a very blank nod and whispered, "Move in on the ranch. The electrified fence, the barbed wire, the concrete wall and the fifty armed men behind that concrete wall."

"Yes. As long as we don't expect to survive, we'll be fine. That's why I'd like you to leave."

She sighed. "OK, but promise me something."

"Yes."

"Yeah, wait. Promise me that you won't get sentimental and tell me your true feelings for me unless there is absolutely no chance of survival. Like, we are both dead, bleeding out, and the air is full of radiation..."

"I get it."

"OK?"

"OK."

We pulled on our goggles. The soldiers were about fifty yards away, now strange warping black silhouettes in a strange green world. She punched my shoulder.

"See you on the other side."

We slid back down the slope and lost ourselves among the ferns, she going one way and I the other, so that we were facing each other across thirty or forty feet of dense undergrowth. If I had not known where she was, she would have been invisible to me. I silently took the bow from my pack, put it together and strung it. And as I fitted the carbon fiber arrow, the small troop appeared over the crest of the hill, amorphous, black and menacing, where Gallin and I had been lying just a couple of minutes before.

They slowed their pace, looking around left to right in the green glow, staying too close together instead of spreading out as they should. I let them move down the slope until the one in the rearguard was level with me, less than thirty feet away. I pulled, aimed with my gut and loosed. The arrow whispered on the air and the razor-sharp steel tip thudded through his temple and punched out the other side.

He never even knew he'd died. He just knelt down and drooped forward. His pals didn't notice, but by then I had knocked another arrow. I stood, drew and loosed and this one punched right through the next guy's back, sliced his heart in half and thudded out through his sternum. The guy standing next to him just stood and stared at the obscene rod poking out of his pal's chest.

By that time it was too late because Gallin had shot him and the guy leading them in the vanguard with her Maxim 9. That left just three. They were very confused and very frightened. My third arrow took out the guy nearest me and sliced clean through his neck. The other two went down with a couple of suppressed double-taps.

She sprinted over and hunkered down beside me. "Nice shooting."

"Back atcha. Let's go for round two."

We left the bodies where they were and moved north around the clearing, leaving a subtle trail, something only a pro would be able to follow, so if one of the other teams was circling around, they'd know where to look for us.

After about ten minutes we started to hear them up ahead, and I began to realize that these were not the pros I had expected, not real pros. These were mercenaries, but they had no real training or discipline. You could hear their boots, and their disgruntled, whining complaints. These guys were speaking Spanish, and from what I could pick up, filtered through the trees, they thought O'Connor was crazy.

We closed in on them silently, and when we were just eight or ten feet from them in that nightmare black and green world, we shot them with the Maxims. It took a fraction under three seconds and the six of them lay dead, free at last from their crazy boss.

The next group came to us, but not as we had expected, from behind. These guys were not competent to track in the forest at night. We heard them as we moved away from the killing field. I glanced at Gallin. She looked like a bug in her helmet with her goggles on. She gave me the thumbs up signifying she had heard them. I had the feeling suddenly that they did not really believe there was anyone in the woods. They had decided O'Connor was crazy, and they were just playing his game and hoping to get well paid for it.

We had come to a narrow track. We moved away from it and took up positions in the blackness. There were two voices approaching, and multiple boots. One of the voices was incessant, whining.

"*Como va a haber un golpe de estado en Estados Unidos, pendejo? El Viejo esta loco, compadre...*"

I knew enough to make out he didn't think there was going to be a coup in the USA, and the old man was crazy. His pal was a wiser man and told him to keep his mouth shut.

"*Calla ya, cojones! Deja de quejarte, vale!*"

He must have carried some interesting thoughts to the grave, mostly about not making assumptions. He was right, the old man was crazy, but it was the crazy old male trying to pull off the coup.

After that we carried on up, following the track through the eerie green world, but keeping in among the trees. After maybe ten minutes, we heard the crackle of a radio. It was hard to make out any detail, but the sounds of muttering voices carried with clarity, seeming almost to be enhanced by the closeness of the woods. Gallin signaled to me that she had eyes on something over on the right. We backed away, separating, in among the tree trunks to where the ferns were thickest. There I picked up a small branch and broke it. The snap was like a gunshot echoing under the canopy. The voices stopped instantly. I nocked an arrow and we waited, motionless and silent.

They took about a minute to come. They were not sure

if what they had heard was a man, or some forest creature. A crack was not enough to call for backup, and they had heard nothing before and nothing since, so they proceeded cautiously, one step at a time, being quiet, listening. They appeared through the green glow, spread out in a line, their weapons cocked and trained forward.

The way they held their rifles made a shot at the heart impossible. A barb through the belly would be a slow, painful death, and a noisy one. This would have to be a headshot. I drew back to my ear, measured the distance, locked my left arm, saw the arrow in my mind hitting its mark and loosed. It happened in less than a second, the soft rattle of the arrow on the wood, the six men frozen, listening for that second sound, the whisper of the feathers though the cool, dark air, and then the cruel thud as the broad, razor-sharp barb rammed home through his eye and shattered the back of his skull.

Gallin was quick. Two double taps: *Phut-phut! Phut-phut!* followed instantly by four eruptions of black-red blood from two of the soldiers. By then I had drawn again and loosed a second arrow which skewered its mark through his back as he turned to run. The last two also tried to run. One made for the trees and Gallin shot him. The other preferred the path, and I feathered his back. Death was instant.

She came up close to me. I said, "Thirty men down. Four at the truck, twenty-six here in the forest. That leaves sixty men, including the guys in the trucks."

"Twenty-four in the trucks, thirty-six inside. How do you want to do it?"

I gripped her wrist in my hand and pulled her close.

"There is a good chance we are going to die tonight,

Gallin. If Nero fails a lot of people will die tonight. I know this sounds weird, but I can't think of anyone I would rather die with."

"Dammit, Mason! You said you weren't going to do that."

"Come on, I have a plan. You'll like this!"

NINETEEN

WE WERE LYING ON OUR BELLIES AT THE EDGE OF the clearing, where we had a clear view of the back of the ranch. It was quiet and very still. The whole area was floodlit so we had removed our goggles and we could see the fence we assumed to be electrified, the field of barbed wire beyond it and the concrete wall. I could also see the cameras mounted on the walls and knew that as soon as we made our assault we would be seen.

I glanced at Gallin but she wasn't looking at me. She jerked her chin toward the far side of the valley. I followed her gaze and saw, about half a mile away, the glow of a procession of headlamps moving along the track among the trees.

"They found the RAM and the bodies. You want we should ambush them as they open the gates?"

I shook my head. "Here's what we do. We have about ten minutes. You position yourself among the trees above the gates. When the gates open, you do an Edward III on them.

Pummel the trucks with grenades, hit the Land Rovers first, they probably have more people in them. Then spray them with automatic fire, and the gate too. We want them to think there is an attack on the gate."

"Meanwhile you...?"

"Meanwhile I am going to take out the nearest cameras, scramble down and plant charges at the base of the electrified fence. I am going to blow it so it falls forward over the barbed wire and provides a ladder up to the top of the wall. With a bit of luck it will short circuit in the fall."

"When I hear the explosions I leg it back to you and we storm the wall together."

"That's the plan. The wall will be our Poitiers. We kill as many as we can, and then we go in and get the president."

She punched my fist. "Good plan. See you in ten."

She crouch-ran back to the cover of the trees and I scrambled down the slope toward the fence. Halfway down I paused to wait. After a minute or two I heard the first grenades explode. I took aim at the nearest cameras mounted on the wall and took them out with a round each.

Then I was running, stumbling and scrambling down the hill again, pulling a cake of C4 from my rucksack as I went. I reached the clearing and sprinted across the grass like I had wings on my heels. I threw myself and made a touchdown at the nearest steel pole, slapped a quarter of a cake of explosive at its base, stabbed in a detonator and ran for the next pole. I could hear a rapid succession of explosions as I went, interspersed with the rattle and chatter of automatic fire. I laid the last charge and sprinted back across the grass to the tree line. There I hurled myself to the ground, pulled out my cell and dialed nine.

There was a moment of absolute stillness. Then there was a horrible smack on the air, a loud flat *bang!* The fence jumped three feet in the air, did a weird snake dance as it was enveloped in dust and smoke and then keeled over and belly-flopped onto the barbed wire.

I already had the assault rifle in my hands with the grenade launcher attached and the magazine rammed home. I didn't wait for Gallin, I roared and charged like a thing demented toward the collapsed fence. I was aware the shooting had stopped and I knew that Gallin was either dead or running for the rendezvous. I pushed the thought from my mind. I had reached the collapsed fence. It was, as I had hoped, leaning against the wall of the ranch. I leapt on to it and scrambled, crab-like, along the mesh toward the top of the wall.

On the far side I could hear all hell and pandemonium breaking loose. I reached the top, lay flat on the fence and peered at the scene of chaos. The gate at the far end of the compound was on fire. I could see at least three trucks burning and numerous bodies scattered in the dirt. There were men running back and forth across the courtyard, screaming and shouting without apparent direction. Some were making for the remaining Land Rovers and Jeeps, others just seemed to be running. I tried to estimate their numbers and decided it was less than fifty. I also decided my first objective was to deny them their trucks, so I lobbed four grenades into the parking area. They exploded, igniting the gas tanks and sending the vehicles dancing and spinning in fiery black silhouettes.

I started to double and triple tap, picking off scrambling soldiers as and when they went. That was when the fence began to bounce and creak. I looked behind me and saw Gallin scrambling up beside me.

"Nice work."

She grinned. "Sitting ducks. How're you making out?"

The yard was clearing. Between us we picked off a couple more soldiers as they ran for cover. I counted the bodies I could see and made it fifteen. A temporary lull settled on the scene.

I said, "I figure he has about fifteen men left, twenty tops. So the question is, what do we do next? I doubt he is going to storm us with fifteen men, but he might try to come behind us."

She nodded. "So we need to strike while they are still confused. Don't allow them to regroup. Where do you figure their weapons are stored?"

"There."

I pointed to a long barn-like prefab. It had large doors that stood closed. Fifty or sixty yards from it, two Land Rovers were moving toward the building. One was moving under its own power, the other, blackened and smoldering, was being pushed by several soldiers who were also using it for cover.

"Let them get to the door and open it. Then cover me."

"What are you going to do? We can take them from here."

"We can take them, but not what's in that barn. Give me your rucksack"

They had pulled up at the door, formed the Land Rovers into a defensive wall, and now opened on us. Gallin lobbed a couple of grenades at them, and opened up. I snatched what I needed from her bag, stuffed it in mine, scrambled and dropped over the wall. I landed on the roof of a small shed, dropped off and rolled.

I scrambled to my feet and charged, spraying the trucks and the soldiers with automatic fire as I went. The trucks rocked, windows shattered and soldiers ducked and scattered under the combined fire. At twenty yards I fired two grenades. I dropped to the ground as they exploded, and as I was showered with scalding dirt, I jumped to my feet and ran for the barn.

Both Land Rovers were smoldering wrecks, littered with scorched bodies. I dodged behind them and threw myself into the barn. There I looked around and saw what I had expected. A vast stockpile of weapons General O'Connor had no doubt been siphoning off from the Army.

I shoved a detonator in one of the eleven cakes of C4 and hurled it in among the huge weapons stash. Then I ran. Only God knows how I made it through the hail of bullets. Gallin did her best to cover me, but one automatic rifle can only suppress a small area at a time.

I managed to make it back to the shed. I blasted the lock on the door, hurled myself in and rolled, as the outside of the building was struck by a hail of fire. Above me the windows imploded and glass sprayed over me under the torrent of burning lead.

Then there were shouts and the shooting stopped. I scrambled to the nearest of the shattered windows and peered out. There was a figure moving among the flames. It was a man, a large man, and he had another man in front of him. As he walked slowly into the courtyard from the house, among the dancing orange light from the flames, the silhouettes of other men began to appear, like creeping stencils above the flame-washed earth.

Then I saw. It was O'Connor, and in front of him, held by the scruff of his neck, was the president. He looked old and frail, with his wispy white hair blowing in the breeze. His steps were uncertain and his hands were held out as though attempting to keep his balance.

"All right, Mason!" O'Connor's voice echoed across the smoldering courtyard. "You made a real mess of things. You and that Mossad bitch are a two-man army. I'm impressed. But it's over. You're too late. Hand yourself in and the president lives. I count to ten and you don't come out, with your hands in the air, and he dies."

I hollered through the broken window, "You kill the president, O'Connor, and it's the last thing you'll ever do. We will blow your head right off."

"I don't think so, Mason."

"And let me remind you, General, that I have just tossed eleven pounds of C4 into your weapons store, which I can detonate at any time. Now I am going to give you one chance to let the president go."

He laughed a big laugh. "You are one of a kind, Mason. You got cojones, no question. But here's the thing. In," he checked his watch, "just over thirty seconds, the Shadow of Death will launch its deadly cargo. One after another they will be propelled into space, to fall toward their targets, and the world will change forever. Thirty seconds, Mason, and it will all be over. You may as well surrender now. There is nothing left for you to do."

"You're bullshitting me." I thought frantically of Nero at Groom Lake. Had they managed it? Had they failed?

Thirty seconds. Was O'Connor right? If we had failed, was there any point in going on? "I could still take you out, you son of a bitch!"

He looked calm, like he had entered some state of grace. He shook his head.

"No need for anybody to die today, Mason. Let me pardon you and your Israeli bitch. All you have to do is come out with your hands up. There will be no Washington DC for you to return to. But you can make a new start in a new, better world." His smile was radiant. "All the major cities, Mason, one after another, until the world returns to sanity. God in his heaven, the kings in their palaces, and the people in their fields."

"O'Connor, can you hear yourself? You're out of your mind!"

"Fifteen seconds..."

He was staring up at the sky. Silence had fallen, but for the crackling of the flames. A gentle breeze had risen. I looked at the president's stricken face. He was trembling in the cold night air. One by one all of them turned their faces up to the night sky. Then General O'Connor's face became transfigured and he raised a trembling hand to point to the heavens. "There," he said and began to laugh, "There! See, there! It is the beginning of the New Order! The dawn of a New Age!"

I got to my feet and staggered out of the shed to look up at the sky. And then I saw it too.

———

Six hundred and fifty miles away Nero pounded the table with his fist. Silence fell around the table and he boomed:

"We have only one option. We are out of time. We have been out of time for hours, and the attack becomes more imminent and more inevitable with every passing minute! So, we cannot target the satellite! It is invisible, so we have *just one option!*"

Rusenko gripped his own hands in despair. "What option, for God's sake?"

Nero pounded the table again. "We must send a *nuclear missile* to the general vicinity of the satellite! As close as Dr. Rusenko's estimates can get it. If the explosion does not destroy the satellite, the EMP will certainly incapacitate it."

Rusenko was shaking his head. "No, no, no! Nero! I told you! The satellite is equipped with lasers. It will detect and target the missile and shoot it down before it…"

"And *that*," interrupted Nero, "is when we will detect it! And have our own laser at the ready! If we are fortunate, they will attempt to reposition the satellite as well, to initiate an attack. Then we will find it, by God!"

Now the brigadier was shaking his head, his hands spread wide. "Have we gone mad here? We can't launch a nuclear missile without the authorization of the president! Besides, we have no nuclear missiles here!"

"Gentlemen!" Nero slammed the table again. "*Gen-tle-men!*" He slammed it one more time for good measure. "We are facing an extinction event! Am I the only person who understands this? *We need a nuclear missile directed at that target!* We needed one ten hours ago! Call Nellis Air Force Base! Get Colonel Rider on the line!"

After some toing and froing Colonel Rider appeared on a screen set into the table. He looked drawn and worried. He addressed the brigadier general.

"General. Good morning. What seems to be the problem?"

"Colonel, are you alone? What I am about to tell you is beyond top secret. You are probably aware that there are questions over the whereabouts of the president..."

"We are hearing rumors, General—"

Nero interrupted. "Get on with it, General! We have no time for this!"

The general sighed and pinched the bridge of his nose. "I am here with the director of ODIN, Dr. Peter Rusenko and Dr. Patel, and I have to tell you that the United States is, as we speak, under imminent threat of nuclear attack from Russia, the president is in a bunker in Montana, and at this very moment there is a satellite, with stealth capability, targeting our major cities, plus London, Brussels, Paris and Berlin."

The colonel had gone waxy pale. He raised his hands, like someone was holding a gun on him. "Sir! Sir, please slow down. What are you telling me?"

"We have no time, Colonel! I need you to respond and step up! We are perhaps minutes from annihilation."

"I cannot act without the authority of the president."

Nero leaned forward. "Colonel Rider, do you know who I am?"

"Yes sir."

"You are getting it direct from Brigadier General Bill Clancy, and from the head of the Office of the Director of Intelligence Networks. The president has disappeared. He may have been abducted. The White House has been compromised and so has the Pentagon. We need to act and we need to act now and we need to act without hesitation, or in just a few minutes we could find America to have been wiped out."

"Jesus..."

The brigadier general spoke up again. "There is no *time* for that, Colonel. You need to make the most important decision of your life. And you need to make the right decision. I am not asking you to strike against Russia, I am *ordering* you to send a missile into space and detonate it at the coordinates that I will give you."

"Into *space?*"

"We are being threatened by a satellite, Colonel, and we need to take that satellite out."

He hesitated for just a moment. Then, "This is a direct order, Brigadier General Clancy?"

"Yes!"

"Very well, sir, if you will send me the coordinates."

Rusenko rattled at a keyboard and sent the coordinates. They were double-checked and Colonel Rider paused for a moment.

"Brigadier General Clancy, am I...?"

"To the best of your knowledge you are obeying orders from a superior officer at a time of unprecedented crisis in national security. I assume full responsibility for the consequences. Fire the missile, Colonel!"

"Yes, sir. If you will stay on the line you can follow the procedure."

The brigadier general snapped. "Stations, everyone! The instant we get a glimpse of that satellite I want it taken out!"

There was a flurry of action as everyone returned to their stations, and the laser cannon was focused on that sector of the sky, now nearing the horizon, where Rusenko had located the satellite.

Nero closed his eyes. In the background he could hear the quiet murmur of instructions and confirmations, both at Groom Lake and at Nellis, where the missile was being positioned. He shut the sounds out of his mind. He knew that from this point on there was nothing he could do. It was out of his hands.

Instead he trod the nightmare path of what happened if they failed to take out the satellite. Chaos would ensue, Russian forces might enter the United States from their bases in the Sea of Okhotsk, via Washington State and Oregon. Would the president emerge from Montana? Was he a prisoner there? Had he been executed? Had there been an invisible coup? And if so, had he that day conducted a counter coup? What steps should he take, and to what extent could he rely on the brigadier general and the colonel?

He was brought out of his reverie by the sound of the colonel's voice, counting down from ten to one. He opened his eyes and saw the colonel's impassive face on the screen, reciting, "Six, five, four..."

He glanced at Rusenko and the laser team gathered about the monitor, staring at the screen.

"Three, two one..."

The tension in the room was palpable. A few people left their posts to roll their chairs to the laser monitor. All eyes were on the sky there, searching for that tiny flash of heat and light.

"Ignition! Fire! Missile away!"

After a moment he turned in his chair to face the screen. "Sir, the missile is launched and on track for its target."

The brigadier general snapped, "Stand by, Colonel." Nero watched him cross the floor to the monitor. The engineer in charge spoke in a monotone. "We have no data, sir. No data...we have...," and then they all erupted, shouting coordinates, pointing, lunging forward. "There! There! On the horizon! Fix it! Fix it!"

The engineer's voice rose above them, steady and calm: "Target acquired and locked, firing in three, two, one. Laser fired."

Then there was a stampede for the hangar doors. The laser engineer stayed at his post. Nero snapped at him, "Fire again, sir! And again!"

Then he rose from his chair and walked, with as much dignity as he could muster, down the spiral stairs and out to the tarmac. He did not see the missile explode. He just heard the gasps of awe, and saw the group of men raise their hands to cover their faces and their eyes as the night sky seemed to glow. Then he saw Rusenko point simultaneously with Patel.

"There!" they said. "See! See the glimmer!" and then, "Oh my God...!"

Nero emerged from the hangar and looked up into the night sky, over to the eastern horizon, and saw, just above Badger Mountain, a bizarre rose formation in the sky, ten or fifteen times the size of the sun, made of brilliant light and fire.

———

AND SIX HUNDRED and fifty miles north I turned to Gallin and gestured her with my hand to back away. Then I pulled my cell and dialed nine. I knew what was coming and I didn't wait. I hurled myself at the general as the first detonation went off. The windows of the weapons deposit erupted in a shower of glass shards. The roof jumped and the walls shook.

I had my Bowie knife in my hand and I slashed savagely into the general's wrist, severing veins and tendons. I snatched the president with my left hand and with my right I plunged the big blade deep into the general's heart. Then I hurled the president onto the ground and fell on top of him as the whole weapons deposit exploded. There was a deafening *bang!* that tore away the walls of the prefab and hurled debris against the walls of the compound, shattering the windows of the ranch and tearing down the outhouses.

I remember thinking it was a miracle I had not been skewered by a shard of wood or a tile. And then there was the roar of flames. I felt the heat all over my back, biting into the skin on my hands and my neck. I could hear screams and terrified shouts and somehow I knew I was going to die.

A hand grabbed me by my burning jacket and dragged me to my feet, screaming, "Son of a bitch! You're on fire!"

I didn't associate the words with the fact that I seemed to be smoking. I bent down, picked up the president and we ran. I don't remember much else, except that we were headed across a cold, dark field. I was carrying the president of the United States and overhead there were bright spotlights, and the thudding of choppers.

EPILOGUE

ALL AROUND THE WORLD PEOPLE RAISED THEIR
eyes to heaven and saw the extraordinary, slowly expanding
phenomenon. Many claimed it was proof of an extraterres-
trial presence in our outer atmosphere. Other believed it was
the start of a long-awaited interplanetary war. Those who
believed in angels claimed it was proof that the level of vibra-
tion of the Earth was rising and we were entering into a new
level of existence. Few guessed it was the first battle of a new
age, fought in space with nuclear weapons and a minimum
of human involvement. The new century, and the new
millennium, had well and truly begun.

Nero, expansive, huge and slightly drunk, refilled
Gallin's glass with champagne, and then refilled mine. His
own was already full.

"I must thank you, Aila, for looking after Alex. I have no
idea what he would have done out there alone." She gave me
a secret wink and he went on. "It is a shame Israel is not in

the Five Eyes, you would be invaluable to us, wouldn't she, Alex?"

"Yes, sir, though I think I did OK, all things considered."

The door opened and Lucas entered with a large silver dish piled high with king prawns garnished with lemon and avocado. Nero smirked, whether at my comment or at the prospect of the prawns was anyone's guess. What he said was:

"Of course the whole thing is being billed as a malfunction in a proposed space station."

"This is what the Kremlin is telling the Russians?"

He nodded. "There was a space station in construction, powered by a radical new Russian nuclear engine. Its purpose was purely scientific, for space exploration. It malfunctioned—probably because of faulty parts supplied by the West—and exploded."

Gallin arched an eyebrow at him. "We are not demanding reparation? They were about to exterminate half the population of the planet."

Nero shrugged and tore the head off a prawn. "The great and the good decided it would be wiser to preserve the peace and not scare the flock. Imagine the consequences if the great, gray mass discovered politicians had been playing with their lives! They agreed to keep quiet, and in exchange it has been revealed that Putin's health is suffering after so many years of caring for his beloved people, and he will be relying more on his advisers and his doctors."

He stuffed the prawn in his mouth and chewed. Gallin said, "So he gets off scot-free."

Nero gave a three-hundred-pound chuckle. "Oh, my dear Aila. If people had the faintest idea of what our politicians get away with." He shook his head, peeling another prawn. "Putin was in many ways the exception because he really does wield an enormous amount of power. He is arguably the richest, most powerful man on Earth. But most politicians, especially the high-profile presidents of the world, are puppets, like film stars. They are given a few years' fame and glory in exchange for doing and saying what they are told."

"Speaking of presidents," I said, sipping the wine and ignoring the prawns, "our own president looked pretty shaken when I carried him out of the ranch."

He nodded without looking at me.

"What you did can't be publicly acknowledged, Alex, you realize that."

"That's not what I'm saying,"

"I know. You will receive a medal, privately, from the president himself. But you understand his health has suffered after the trauma of these events, and for a time he will be leaving the day-to-day running of the country in the hands of his advisors."

I arched an eyebrow which he also ignored. "Not Andy Costello, we trust."

"There are a lot of lessons to be learned from what has happened, Alex. And we are all busy learning them. But there is a curious irony, here."

Gallin was busily shelling prawns and eating them, but looked up now and said, "Irony?"

He nodded. "There are those who are saying that this happened because increasingly these gigantic political power blocks, like Russia and China, are governed by single person-alities, like Putin, who have gathered far too much power into their own hands. So much power, the theory goes, leads to madness. And we find suddenly that the madness of one man has infected the whole planet!"

I sipped and shrugged. "Makes sense to me. Isn't that what happened?"

"Indeed. But then there is the other argument." He spread his hands. "What happened here? Power was spread over so many institutions: the White House, the Pentagon, Congress, the CIA, ODIN, that when the president was duped and effectively kidnapped, the federal government became a headless chicken. Had the president been less of a figurehead—less of a tool for his party—and more of a Washington, a Roosevelt or a Kennedy, this might never have happened."

"Do you believe that?" I asked.

He sat back and stared at me. I realized it was the first time he had looked at me all evening. He had his glass halfway to his mouth and sat licking his lips. He sipped his wine and set the glass carefully down on the table.

"For reasons that are far too complex to go into now, Alex, I believe this world is fatally flawed. We shall none of us go to hell, do you know why?" He didn't let me answer. He plowed on. "Because we are already there. As Milton tells us, the mind is its own place, and can make a heaven of hell, and a hell of heaven. The purpose of politicians, Alex, is to accrue power by whatever means and at any cost. They will make a hell of heaven. We, at ODIN, have the mission of keeping them in check."

Gallin sat back, drained her glass and failed to suppress a quiet belch.

"So let me see if I have got this straight," she said. "Putin, riding high on his enormous power, commissioned the construction of this satellite."

"That was a few years back," I said.

"Right, and nobody in his cabinet dared tell him he was out of his mind. Partly because most of them were as crazy as he was, and the others feared for their lives if they crossed him."

Nero nodded. "Correct."

I sipped. "I guess at first it was no more crazy than having nuclear missiles in silos on the planet. But as the project grew, and he realized the USA had nothing to match it, he started going even crazier than he was already. The problem was, there was nothing to stop him."

Nero said, "And when the time came to launch the damn thing, all he could see over here in the White House and in the Pentagon, was a bunch of people who were willing to compromise on just about anything to preserve the peace. We were negotiating with Iran, Russia, Chin..." He spluttered. "The field effectively belonged to whomsoever was willing to take it by force. And he was that man."

Gallin went on. "So when Rusenko saw that his Shadow of Death was actually being armed and launched, he made his plans with his pal Patel, and arranged to come and give the launch codes and the coordinates to the USA, so they could stop the satellite."

Nero refilled her glass. "Exactly. However, what we did not know was that Putin was playing a very subtle game. He did not want simply to blow the USA off the map. No, he wanted to extend his empire all the way around the globe. He *wanted* the USA for himself. He was to be the greatest emperor in history.

"He achieved this by selecting an American general who was hawkish and aggressive, perhaps too much so, and had been passed over a few times for important posts, and felt resentful and bitter. Approaches were made and friendships forged with influential Russians. Naturally as his apparent influence in Russia grew, his stock at the White House grew, and with a few words planted here and there and a few strings pulled, Putin soon had his man right next to the president." He shrugged. "After that it was just a matter of promises of riches and power, a key position in the New World Order, finally eliminating the sickness and the corruption from the system." He paused, considering his glass. "What he said to me when I interrogated him was, 'By the time I realized it was crazy and had gone too far, it was too late. All I could do was go with it, and hope Putin was powerful enough to pull it off.'"

Gallin studied her empty glass and slid it across the table to Nero. "Men like Putin," she said, "are infectious. Their madness is contagious. You meet them and you see a head of state, with a vast office and control over entire nations. Everybody obeys them and they are supported by the state. They cannot be mad, because the entire nation depends on them and buys into their narrative. So when they tell you, you can be the next head of state in your country if you pay homage to me, you believe them."

"Sadly, that is true, Aila. We see it over and over again." He sighed. "So, when we were informed that Rusenko wanted to defect, the first thing I did was inform the president, and the first thing he did was consult with General O'Connor, who immediately reported back to the Kremlin. With the Kremlin's agreement and cooperation, he put the matter in the hands of Colonel James Gordon, who fortunately for us, made a hash of the operation, but not before torturing and killing poor Mira."

Gallin asked, "So, the president was never a part of this?"

I shook my head. "Never. O'Connor tried hard to make it look like he was, but he wasn't. They gulled him, lied to him and confused him, but he was never a part of it, except as a victim."

Lucas returned and took away the dish of empty prawn shells and our plates. He returned a few moments later with another silver dish containing sirloin steaks cooked in cream and pepper sauce with cognac. There were also new potatoes in butter and parsley, Vichy carrots and fresh sweet peas. The wine was an '82 Muga.

When Lucas had left, Nero gave me that strange look again.

"How are your burns, by the way, and your shoulder?"

I gave him a smile that was on the skinny side of thin. "Not bad, nothing a month's holiday in the Caribbean can't cure."

He nodded. "Good. I think you've earned it. What do you say, Aila?"

She smiled at me and winked. "I think he's earned it too."

"Fine, that's settled then. Your very good health."

LATER THAT NIGHT, at about two in the morning, Gallin dropped me off outside my house on Adams Street. I opened the door and she reached out and took my hand.

"Mason—"

I looked back, a little surprised. "What?"

"You going to be OK?"

"Sure." I smiled. "I have Manny Pacquiao to look after me."

She closed her eyes and smiled. When she opened them again she said, "Where are you going to go?"

"To bed?"

"I mean on your holiday, asshole."

"Oh, I don't know. I said the Caribbean, but actually I could do with something a bit quieter. Two weeks in a luxury hotel in Maine, reading, feeding and drinking by an open fire sounds good. And then two weeks at home, reading the paper, reading books, taking it easy."

She nodded a lot, still smiling. "I told my dad I needed some time off too. It was pretty stressful."

"You coped admirably. I don't know what I would have done."

"Thanks. So, I'm not sure what to do..."

We smiled at each other for a little too long. Then I grinned and she grinned. "Why don't you join me in Maine?" I said, "And we'll see how much trouble we can get into."

"Let's discuss it over breakfast," she said, and gave me a peck on the cheek.

I got out and watched her car drive away. As I climbed the steps to my front door, I could see Manny Pacquiao watching me through the bay window. He looked pissed. I was in trouble for sure.

Don't miss RUSSIAN ROULETTE. The riveting sequel in the Alex Mason Thriller series.

Scan the QR code below to purchase RUSSIAN ROULETTE.

Or go to: righthouse.com/russian-roulette

NOTE: flip to the very end to read an exclusive sneak peak...

DON'T MISS ANYTHING!

If you want to stay up to date on all new releases in this series, with these authors, or with any of our new deals, you can do so by joining our newsletters below.

In addition, you will immediately gain access to our entire *Right House VIP Library,* which currently includes *ORIGINS*—a full length prequel novel to *ODIN.*

righthouse.com/email

(Easy to unsubscribe. No spam. Ever.)

ALSO BY DAVID ARCHER

Up to date books can be found at:
www.righthouse.com/david-archer

ROGUE THRILLERS
Gates of Hell (Book 1)
Hell's Fury (Book 2)

JACOB HUNTER THRILLERS
The Kyiv File (Book 1)
The Bogota File (Book 2)

PETER BLACK THRILLERS
Burden of the Assassin (Book 1)
The Man Without A Face (Book 2)
Unpunished Deeds (Book 3)
Hunter Killer (Book 4)
Silent Shadows (Book 5)
The Last Run (Book 6)
Dark Corners (Book 7)
Ghost Operative (Book 8)

ALEX MASON THRILLERS
Odin (Book 1)
Ice Cold Spy (Book 2)
Mason's Law (Book 3)
Assets and Liabilities (Book 4)
Russian Roulette (Book 5)

Executive Order (Book 6)
Dead Man Talking (Book 7)
All The King's Men (Book 8)
Flashpoint (Book 9)
Brotherhood of the Goat (Book 10)
Dead Hot (Book 11)
Blood on Megiddo (Book 12)
Son of Hell (Book 13)

NOAH WOLF THRILLERS

Code Name Camelot (Book 1)
Lone Wolf (Book 2)
In Sheep's Clothing (Book 3)
Hit for Hire (Book 4)
The Wolf's Bite (Book 5)
Black Sheep (Book 6)
Balance of Power (Book 7)
Time to Hunt (Book 8)
Red Square (Book 9)
Highest Order (Book 10)
Edge of Anarchy (Book 11)
Unknown Evil (Book 12)
Black Harvest (Book 13)
World Order (Book 14)
Caged Animal (Book 15)
Deep Allegiance (Book 16)
Pack Leader (Book 17)
High Treason (Book 18)
A Wolf Among Men (Book 19)
Rogue Intelligence (Book 20)
Alpha (Book 21)

Rogue Wolf (Book 22)
Shadows of Allegiance (Book 23)
In the Grip of Darkness (Book 24)

SAM PRICHARD MYSTERIES
The Grave Man (Book 1)
Death Sung Softly (Book 2)
Love and War (Book 3)
Framed (Book 4)
The Kill List (Book 5)
Drifter: Part One (Book 6)
Drifter: Part Two (Book 7)
Drifter: Part Three (Book 8)
The Last Song (Book 9)
Ghost (Book 10)
Hidden Agenda (Book 11)

SAM AND INDIE MYSTERIES
Aces and Eights (Book 1)
Fact or Fiction (Book 2)
Close to Home (Book 3)
Brave New World (Book 4)
Innocent Conspiracy (Book 5)
Unfinished Business (Book 6)
Live Bait (Book 7)
Alter Ego (Book 8)
More Than It Seems (Book 9)
Moving On (Book 10)
Worst Nightmare (Book 11)
Chasing Ghosts (Book 12)
Serial Superstition (Book 13)

CHANCE REDDICK THRILLERS
Innocent Injustice (Book 1)
Angel of Justice (Book 2)
High Stakes Hunting (Book 3)
Personal Asset (Book 4)

CASSIE MCGRAW MYSTERIES
What Lies Beneath (Book 1)
Can't Fight Fate (Book 2)
One Last Game (Book 3)
Never Really Gone (Book 4)

ALSO BY BLAKE BANNER

Up to date books can be found at:
www.righthouse.com/blake-banner

ROGUE THRILLERS
Gates of Hell (Book 1)
Hell's Fury (Book 2)

ALEX MASON THRILLERS
Odin (Book 1)
Ice Cold Spy (Book 2)
Mason's Law (Book 3)
Assets and Liabilities (Book 4)
Russian Roulette (Book 5)
Executive Order (Book 6)
Dead Man Talking (Book 7)
All The King's Men (Book 8)
Flashpoint (Book 9)
Brotherhood of the Goat (Book 10)
Dead Hot (Book 11)
Blood on Megiddo (Book 12)
Son of Hell (Book 13)

HARRY BAUER THRILLER SERIES
Dead of Night (Book 1)
Dying Breath (Book 2)
The Einstaat Brief (Book 3)

Quantum Kill (Book 4)
Immortal Hate (Book 5)
The Silent Blade (Book 6)
LA: Wild Justice (Book 7)
Breath of Hell (Book 8)
Invisible Evil (Book 9)
The Shadow of Ukupacha (Book 10)
Sweet Razor Cut (Book 11)
Blood of the Innocent (Book 12)
Blood on Balthazar (Book 13)
Simple Kill (Book 14)
Riding The Devil (Book 15)
The Unavenged (Book 16)
The Devil's Vengeance (Book 17)
Bloody Retribution (Book 18)
Rogue Kill (Book 19)
Blood for Blood (Book 20)

DEAD COLD MYSTERY SERIES
An Ace and a Pair (Book 1)
Two Bare Arms (Book 2)
Garden of the Damned (Book 3)
Let Us Prey (Book 4)
The Sins of the Father (Book 5)
Strange and Sinister Path (Book 6)
The Heart to Kill (Book 7)
Unnatural Murder (Book 8)
Fire from Heaven (Book 9)
To Kill Upon A Kiss (Book 10)
Murder Most Scottish (Book 11)

The Butcher of Whitechapel (Book 12)
Little Dead Riding Hood (Book 13)
Trick or Treat (Book 14)
Blood Into Wine (Book 15)
Jack In The Box (Book 16)
The Fall Moon (Book 17)
Blood In Babylon (Book 18)
Death In Dexter (Book 19)
Mustang Sally (Book 20)
A Christmas Killing (Book 21)
Mommy's Little Killer (Book 22)
Bleed Out (Book 23)
Dead and Buried (Book 24)
In Hot Blood (Book 25)
Fallen Angels (Book 26)
Knife Edge (Book 27)
Along Came A Spider (Book 28)
Cold Blood (Book 29)
Curtain Call (Book 30)

THE OMEGA SERIES
Dawn of the Hunter (Book 1)
Double Edged Blade (Book 2)
The Storm (Book 3)
The Hand of War (Book 4)
A Harvest of Blood (Book 5)
To Rule in Hell (Book 6)
Kill: One (Book 7)
Powder Burn (Book 8)
Kill: Two (Book 9)
Unleashed (Book 10)

ABOUT US

Right House is an independent publisher created by authors for readers. We specialize in Action, Thriller, Mystery, and Crime novels.

If you enjoyed this novel, then there is a good chance you will like what else we have to offer! Please stay up to date by using any of the links below.

Join our mailing lists to stay up to date -->
righthouse.com/email
Visit our website --> righthouse.com
Contact us --> contact@righthouse.com

 facebook.com/righthousebooks
 x.com/righthousebooks
 instagram.com/righthousebooks

EXCLUSIVE SNEAK PEAK OF...

RUSSIAN ROULETTE

PROLOGUE

José Fernandez had never known his wife to do anything remarkable. Had her life been a golf course, she would have been exactly par. She was quite pretty (she might have been beautiful if she had had some remarkable feature on her face), she had black hair and dark eyes and regular features, she was neither fat nor thin and she had all the right curves in all the right places; but not in a way you would ever notice.

Her personality was much like her looks. She was charming, never really got more than annoyed, never got depressed, was never excessively happy. She might have been adorable or fascinating, only she was never extreme enough to achieve either state. Of course that made her ideal for a job as a civil servant—a post which, in Spain, glories in the name of "functionary." The name was appropriate because that was exactly what Maria Garcia Orcera, José's wife, did at the Malaga City Hall: she functioned.

Maria had once seen a documentary on Spanish TV about the sea squirt. The narrator had described it as a creature which starts its life cycle as a predator, eventually finds a rock, or a solid place to which it attaches itself, then proceeds to eat its own brain and become a vegetable. "And in this sense," said the narrator, "it is very similar to a functionary."

That had amused her a lot, though she had not shown it.

In her professional life she never missed a day at work, she never arrived late, she never left work unfinished and never did it badly. Neither did she stay a second past three PM, nor did she produce work that was good enough to be noticed. She was, in four words, an unremarkable sea squirt.

And that was exactly what José had always loved so much about her (he being also a functionary). In fact it was what all their friends loved about her: She was utterly predictable. Which was why it was so deeply unsettling when, in early April, Maria announced that they were taking two weeks off in May. They were due the time, she told him, and she had already arranged it with both of their heads of department. And, as if this were not disturbing enough, she then compounded his dismay by turning up late after work driving a brand new Audi A4 sedan.

They had stood on the sidewalk and she had hugged him and grinned while he shook his head and looked alarmed.

"Are you crazy? How are we going to pay for it? Where are we going to park it? I already have a car. *You* have a car. You're crazy!"

She had told him not to be silly and she had kissed him a lot (which just made the whole thing even more bizarre). "I won the lottery!" she said, "I didn't tell you because I wanted it to be a surprise. I've always wanted an Audi, haven't you? And there's more!"

"Lottery? Nobody wins the lottery. More? You know I don't like surprises."

"We're going on holiday!"

"Holiday? Where? When? Why? It's not summer yet."

"May! José, I *told* you we were taking two weeks in May!"

"But I thought..." he said and went and peered into the car through the tinted windows. "I thought we'd stay at home or go to Cadiz for a week..."

"*José...!*" She made a pouting face, knowing he could never resist that. "You are spoiling everything!"

"It's just... It's unexpected. How much do we have to pay every month for this?" He opened the door and gazed at the controls.

"I *told* you! Nothing! It's paid for!"

He looked up at her and winced. "And the holiday?"

"Nothing!" She laughed. "It's paid for! Aren't you even going to ask where we're going?"

It hadn't occurred to him because he didn't really want to know. "Where?" he asked with more anxiety than curiosity. He was still hunkered down by the car door and she hunkered down beside him. He glanced at her face. Her eyes were brighter than normal and she seemed to have more teeth, and they were whiter. He had never seen her like this and was wondering if it would all lead in the end to a divorce. "We are going," she said, "*to Belarus!*"

He made a face as though his mother-in-law had just told him they were having toad's brains for dinner. It was a mix of distress and incomprehension, a kind of facial *why?*

"*Belarus?* Where is that? Isn't that near Russia? Aren't we at war with them?"

"Of course not! We are going to the beautiful city of Minsk!"

He stood. "I thought Minsk was in Russia."

"It's the capital of Belarus, between Poland, Russia and Ukraine."

"You're crazy! What's wrong with you? What's happened to you? Ukraine? We are going on holiday to a country that's between Russia and Ukraine? You're mad!"

She dismissed his anxiety with the same ease with which she dismissed almost everything about him. A brief, "Oh, come on!" was sufficient, though for good measure she added, "The war is miles away!" and illustrated this by lifting her hands, as though she were holding a map, and saying, "Look, we are here, in Minsk," and she pointed at imaginary Minsk with her finger, "And the fighting is all the way down here," she pointed to a distant spot which was presumably the southeastern area of Donbas and Mariupol.

He narrowed his eyes at her. They seemed to ask, *What have you done with the real Maria Garcia?* and she followed up with, "Come! Let me show you the car. You'll love it! We'll take it for a drive and have lunch in Fuengirola."

She climbed behind the wheel and he got in the passenger side. "What's in Minsk?" he asked as the engine hummed impressively and they moved off.

"*Joder, Pepe!*" she said—which translates exactly to, "Fuck, Pepe!" but in tone and quality is more like, "Jesus, Pepe!" because the Spanish curse and swear copiously and fluently from an early age, and think nothing of it—"It's known for…um…abundant Soviet-era architecture, the Bolshoi Ballet Theatre, odd things like a Cat Museum, whose director is called Donut the Cat. Also there are primeval forests, incredible landscapes, the food is great…"

"A cat museum."

"Yes, darling."

"And the director is a cat—"

"Yes, darling, a cat called Donut. You'll love it. You'll see. We'll drive."

He was staring out of the window, shaking his head. Eventually he turned to face her. They were speeding along the highway, far above the glistening Mediterranean, racing past Benalmadena, with its Buddhist Stupa and the Butterfly Museum, but he saw none of that.

"What has happened to you, *cariño*? Are you in love? Is there somebody else? Are you having a midlife crisis? Is it a premature menopause? Tell me. We'll discuss it and get through it together. But please, stop this madness."

She laughed out loud and smacked his knee. "Don't be so *tonto*, José! We could use a holiday! Go somewhere different! See something different! Try new food, stay in a nice hotel. It will be wonderful, you'll see. And it won't cost us a penny!"

He didn't say anything to his wife. He just stared at her as she sped down the highway, weaving from lane to lane, overtaking the other, slower cars. He had never known his wife to drive so fast before. It was all part of that strange and unsettling day.

They went to La Carihuela on the seafront, and ate outside on the terrace. He ordered a small beer and she ordered glass of cold white wine, and while the waiter went to get their drinks she leaned across the table and covered his hand with hers.

"You know what I have been wanting for a long time?"

"What?" he asked her, with an unhappy feeling of dread in his belly as images of babies, dirty nappies and sleepless nights loomed in his imagination.

"A paella!"

He sighed with relief and breathed more easily. "Yes! Yes, paella. We should do that. We'll tell Emilio and Rosario to join us, and Juan and Rosa. We'll go to the *chiringuito* on the beach, one Sunday, maybe in July..."

He trailed off because she was smiling and shaking her head. "Now. I want it *now!*"

He narrowed his eyes, spread his hands, shrugged. It was a very Mediterranean gesture. "You have to order in advance. You know that. You order Friday or Saturday for Sunday. It takes a couple of hours to make..."

He trailed off because she was shaking her head again.

"I ordered it this morning from the office."

"You knew. You knew then that we were coming."

"I've known since April."

"You've booked the hotel in Minsk, too, haven't you?" She nodded and sipped. "How much did you win on the lottery, Maria? Maybe you should have told me, you know?"

"Sixty." He looked down at his cutlery and spent some time adjusting and straightening it. "Sixty thousand euros." He nodded, shrugged, looked up at her and nodded again. "You know, maybe you should have—it's a lot of money. Maybe you should have told...told..."

"What for? This is what I wanted to spend the money

on, José, and I am giving you the opportunity to enjoy it with me. Don't be ungrateful. Relax and enjoy it."

His mouth pinched into a prim beak. He reached for his beer and sipped it, leaving only the tiniest trace of foam on his upper lip.

"You seem different," he said. She picked up an olive and put it in her mouth, chewed watching him but said nothing. "When are we going, then? I'll have to pack. And we'll have to tell Emilio and Rosario, and Juan and Rosa. They're going to think you've gone crazy."

"*Cariño*," she dropped the olive stone in the saucer, "sometimes people go a little bit crazy. It's part of being normal." She gave a small laugh. "It's how we know we *are* normal, because we are doing something exceptional. You're forty, I'm thirty-five, and what have we ever done that was crazy or wild or exciting?"

He shrugged. "I have never done anything crazy or wild or exciting. Why would I? You, I don't know. You never tell me about your past. I always thought you were like me. But today, all of this..." He shook his head.

She sighed, aware she was taking the wrong tack with him. She reached across the table for his hand.

"We've been married five years, José. And for me they have been five very happy years. You have given my life stability." She nodded and after a moment repeated, "Stability. But just this once, *cariño*, just once, I would like to go on this little adventure. I am paying for everything with my money. We are perfectly safe, everything is as it should be. We just get in the car, drive across Europe, visit Minsk and come home. It will make me very, very happy. It will be something to tell our grandchildren about, if we ever get crazy enough to have children."

Nothing perceptible happened on her face. The smile was there, all her facial muscles were in the same place, but somehow the eyes went hard and cold, and all the warmth evaporated from her expression.

"You love me, don't you, José?" Her voice had become flat and mechanical. "You don't want to make me unhappy, do you?"

"No."

"I would be *very* unhappy if we didn't go tomorrow."

"No, no, that's not what I..."

The warmth flooded back and she squeezed his hand. "It would make me *so* happy. It would mean so much to me. You are such a good, supportive husband. You are my rock, *cariño*."

"It's just so sudden. So unexpected..."

She lifted his hand with both of hers and kissed it. "*Cariño*," she said, "it will be wonderful, we'll go via Barcelona, France, Switzerland, Germany, the Czech Republic, Poland and finally, Belarus—"

"*Dios mío!* How far is that?"

"Three thousand one hundred and thirty kilometers.[1]"

"More than *three thousand kilometers?*"

For a moment it seemed to him that her eyes lost all their humanity. If asked to put the feeling into words he would not have been able to, but it was as though, in her eyes, he saw her capacity for empathy shut down, as though the fuse had been removed, and her humanity had died.

"Six thousand kilometers there and back, my love, and I need you there by my side, happy and enjoying the adventure. Because if you don't, I will have to kill you and take somebody else."

They stared at each other for a long count of five, then her face creased and she burst out laughing. For a moment he did not laugh with her, but after a second his gape turned into a smile, and through sheer relief he too began to laugh.

"You had me worried!"

She nodded, still laughing. "Good!"

The paella arrived and was placed in the center of the table. José ordered another beer and rose to go to the bathroom. While she was alone Maria pulled her cell from her bag and called a number she had listed as "travel agents." It rang once and was answered immediately by a woman with a voice like sandpaper.

"Yes?"

"I think we are OK. He is very shocked, but I think he will adjust."

"Is he going to start talking to all his friends about your strange behavior? We cannot have that."

"I know, Colonel, but he will be with me at every moment. We will depart early tomorrow—"

"At what time?"

"Six AM. And he will see no one before that."

"Is it necessary to eliminate him and replace him?"

"No. It is safer this way. Perhaps on the return."

"Good. Keep me informed. There can be no mistakes, Maria."

"I know, Colonel. There will be no mistakes."

José came back from the bathroom and as he sat down she gazed at him with fond eyes and sighed, "*Ay, mi Pepe!*" She reached for his hand as he tried to pick up his fork, and turned that into a joke so that they both laughed. Then she started reminiscing about how they had met, and all the funny things that had happened to them up to the time they got married. Before long he was joining in, talking about how amazing it was that they had both passed their civil service exams with flying colors and both managed to land jobs in City Hall in Malaga.

"I never thought it could happen," he said. "I thought I'd get a moderately good pass. But you, you were so sure, so confident, as though you *knew*."

"I did," she said simply. "It had to be. We had to be together. It was destiny." That, she thought, and the fact that the Russian Mafia owned City Hall in Malaga.

A couple of hours later she made him drive the Audi back home, telling him he had to get used to the car. She praised him at every opportunity, as though she were a little drunk, though she had had only half a glass of wine, and when they got home she dragged him to the bedroom and blew his mind.

While he slept she packed their cases and put their travel documents into her bag. Then she sat on the balcony with a gin and tonic and watched the sun set fire to the western horizon. On clear days like this you could see the black silhouettes of the Atlas Mountains in Africa, rising above the blood-red horizon. Africa and Europe, she thought, dead and dying empires. Soon the world would see a new empire, the greatest empire in history, and all others, the Chinese, the Europeans, the British and especially the Americans, would bow down before them.

The long winter of the Cold War was over, the great Bear was stirring, waking from hibernation. She smiled at the metaphor. It pleased her. Soon the Russian Bear would wake and roar. And, she thought, what would set it aside from all other empires was not its military might, though it was mighty indeed. No, it was its willingness to *use* that might, to visit hell and devastation on its enemies, without flinching. That was what set Russia aside from its enemies.

The hibernation was over, the Bear was awake.

CHAPTER 1

AT ABOUT THE TIME THAT MARIA AND JOSÉ WERE crossing the Rhine from Altstadt in Switzerland to Konstanz in Germany, I was getting bored and drunk in Miami. I'd had about as much beach and pool as a man can take, and I was sitting in Jack Dusty's at the Ritz-Carlton in Sarasota. I was sipping my fourth martini and contemplating the word, "pinguid." It was a good word. It meant fatty, oily, greasy, unctuous. There was a guy sitting a couple of tables away talking to a high-class hooker who had brought the word into my mind. And that got me to thinking about taking early retirement, growing a beard and settling somewhere where I could write my memoirs, and use words like "pinguid." I figured I'd be the kind of writer who used a lot of alliteration. I'd create characters like Pinguid Pete, the greasiest don in Jersey, or Odontos Osmanek, the Cannibal of Constantinople.

I drained my glass, considered its emptiness for a moment, and wondered what Gallin was doing at that moment. The thought of Gallin made me decide I should probably not have another. I raised my hand to call the waiter and order a refill, when my cell rang. It was the distinctive ring of the office, so I sighed and pulled my phone from my pocket. Lovelock's voice oozed like pinguid hot chocolate in my ear.

"Hi sweetheart, Nero wants you to see the news, right now. Then get your skinny white ass to Bradenton Airport. There will be a plane waiting for you."

"If I do, will you dine with me tonight, Lovelock?"

"Sure I will, Mason. You just close your eyes and think of me. It'll be just like I was there, in the flesh..."

I sighed and went up to my suite. There I switched to the news channel, and sobered up fast. Kate O'Connor was standing outside the White House talking into the camera.

"...Jim, the word from the White House is that this is a hoax. A source very close to the president told me, in no uncertain terms, that this was, and I quote, 'bovine excrement.' But the rumors on social media persist. And so far all the major newspapers and broadcasters have received identical information, from a source identifying itself as the Russian Executive for the Dissemination of Sovietism—"

Jim's voice cut in and asked, "Kate, let me just stop you there for a moment, but the acronym for this name would be of course REDS. REDS, Soviets, these are terms we have not heard since the Cold War..."

"Yes, and that's partly why the White House and the Pentagon are being pretty dismissive of it. However, what Republican spokesman Mitch Bannon said to me, just a few minutes ago, was that Moscow has been showing ever stronger Soviet leanings in recent years, and that there are many in the Kremlin who favor a return to a more Soviet style of government. And he has a point, Jim. You just need to look at the recent invasion of Ukraine. The word among Republicans, and among the more hawkish Democrats, is that it would be a mistake to dismiss the claims of the REDS out of hand."

Jim's voice came back. "Kate, does this so-called Russian Executive claim to be connected in any way to the Kremlin or the Russian Government?"

"No such claim has been made, Jim. Neither has it been denied. From what I understand—and I stress this has *not* been confirmed—the president has telephoned Mr. Putin personally and demanded an explanation. Mr. Putin has categorically denied that the REDS organization has anything to do with them. It is, according to the Kremlin, a minor terrorist organization that by no stretch of the imagination has the resources to back up its claims."

"Kate, on the subject of those claims. Now, we are getting mixed, garbled messages, mainly from social media, about what the REDS claim to have done, or claim to be doing—can you shed any light on that?"

"Yes, Jim. We have an official statement from the Pentagon. It confirms that the Russian Executive for the Dissemination of Sovietism claims to have placed, or are in the process of placing, six TNDs—"

"TNDs, Kate, tell us what those are."

"TNDs, Jim, are tactical nuclear devices. Not to be confused with tactical nuclear weapons or warheads. The TND is essentially a small, portable nuclear bomb in a suitcase or a rucksack. It was first developed by the United States as far back as the late 1950s, when it was known as the W54.

"There have been major concerns about the existence and whereabouts of Soviet TNDs since the collapse of the Soviet Union, Jim, and it seems on May 30th, 1997 a congressional delegation met with General Aleksandr Lebed, the former Secretary of the Russian Security Council. During that meeting, General Lebed told the delegation he was aware that at least eighty-four of these portable nuclear devices had gone missing."

"That is extremely worrying."

"Yes, Jim, and in September of that same year, Lebed went on to state in interviews with CBS and *Sixty Minutes*, that the Russian military had lost more than a hundred out of a total of 250 'suitcase nuclear bombs.' He said specifically in those interviews that the devices were designed to look exactly like suitcases. So, Jim, we know that the devices exist, and we know that at least a hundred of them went missing amid the chaos of the collapse of the Soviet Union, over twenty years ago."

"That is pretty terrifying news, Kate. And now the REDS are claiming they have planted or are planting..."

"Six, at various locations around the United States. But here is the weird twist, Jim. They claim that five of the six are dummies, and only one is real, with the capacity to take out an entire medium-sized city. But, the discovery of any one of them, or the attempt to deactivate any one of them, *might* trigger the real bomb..."

I switched off the TV, had a strong, black coffee and packed my bags.

———

WHEN WE TOUCHED down at Ronald Reagan Airport there was a limo waiting which took me straight to the Commonwealth Tower on Wilson Boulevard. Ten minutes later I was admitted to Office 1I in what we fondly called Valhalla, Nero's inner sanctum. As the door closed behind me I sat in the chair across from him. He regarded me with eyes which were set in a face that was distinctly pinguid, but held all the menace of an impending storm.

"Well?" he said.

"The White House says it's bovine excrement. Is it?"

"It is neither bovine excrement nor equine excrement. And there will be no cover to be had anywhere if it hits the fan," he replied, stretching the metaphor to the breaking point. "Facts!" he snapped. "The Russian Executive for the Dissemination of Sovietism has contacted not only the social and news media, they have also directly contacted the CIA, the FBI, Military Intelligence at the Pentagon and the president at the White House. They assert that tactical nuclear devices capable of destroying a medium-sized city have been placed, or are being placed, at six locations…" He trailed off and arched an eyebrow because I was shaking my head. "No?" he asked.

"What is that," I said, "'have been placed, or are being placed'? What does that mean? They've been placed or they haven't."

"This whole enterprise, Alex, is about unsettling and unnerving, and attempting to provoke a state of chaos. The stock market crash of '29 did more damage to this country than either of the World Wars or the Cold War, and that was triggered by uncertainty and chaos. So, to engender that uncertainty and chaos they tell us that the devices have been placed, or are in the process of being placed. They will not tell us which. Equally, they do not tell us *where* they have been placed, or which is the authentic one."

"OK, I get that. They want to create an environment of uncertainty. But wouldn't it have been more effective, if they have a hundred of these damned suitcase devices, to plant six actual, real bombs?"

"No, Alex, because if six nuclear devices were detonated in the United States, then the country would be largely uninhabitable. And that is in nobody's interest. Also, if it is a risk to bring one nuclear device into the country, that risk is exponentially greater if you multiply it by six, because each discovery upon crossing customs increases the possibility that the other five will also be found. This way, five dummies can be made *in situ*, while only one need be smuggled in. And the uncertainty across the country caused by the fear of that single nuclear device, as it escalates toward fever pitch, will cause maximum economic damage while causing minimal logistical damage."

"That is subtle to the point of being fiendish."

"Fiendish." He nodded. "Indeed."

"And, from what I hear, finding and defusing them, whether they are dummies or not, could detonate the genuine one."

"That is what they have told us. Whether it is true or not, or some variation of the truth, we cannot know." He slipped a piece of paper across the desk. "They have given us these locations." I picked up the paper and read it aloud.

"Texas, New Mexico, Los Angeles, Washington DC, Silicon Valley and New York." I studied them a moment while Nero studied me. Finally I said, "Logic dictates that we should ignore this list on the basis that why the hell would they tell us where they were putting their bomb?" I shook my head. "But it's a double bluff. These locations make perfect sense. Texas: the oil fields. New Mexico: the Groom Lake facility and our most advanced military technology. Los Angeles: Hollywood: a major source of revenue, and our major propaganda machine. Washington DC: obviously because they would knock out our government and military HQ. Silicon Valley because it's Silicon Valley and some of the most advanced AI and IT research on the planet is there, and New York because it is the economic driver of the nation. They all make perfect sense as major targets."

"I agree."

"And if my purpose were to cripple the country politically and economically—"

"Alex," he raised a hand, "work it the other way. A process of elimination. Tell me what you would *not* do."

I frowned and scratched my ear. "OK, I would *not* nuke Texas. Because when the economy collapses I want to buy Texas, or at least its oil wells and its beef. The same logic applies to California as a whole and Silicon Valley in particular. There is technology there I would want for me. Again, the same applies to New Mexico. If they aim to destroy our economy, it's so they can move in, buy into our infrastructure and take possession of our technology and our resources."

"Good. So...?"

"So the two that stand out then as targets are Washington and New York. One for the political damage it will cause and the other for the economic damage."

He was nodding. "Exactly, but if you take out DC it is as

though you had dropped a bomb on New York at the same time. The collateral damage to the stock exchange would sink the economy overnight. Every major investor in the world would sell like crazy and pull his money out of the USA within hours. Within a day the country would be virtually bankrupted."

"So you think DC is the target? Isn't it too obvious?"

"Another double bluff. We are guaranteed to think it is too obvious and turn to New York or Texas as the more subtle targets. But Washington is the big prize, and let's face it, it is the one place where the actual physical, logistical damage is least. In fact some of the collateral damage is useful to them. The FBI on E Street, Norfolk, Arlington, us. We would all suffer terminal damage. Our capacity to govern, our capacity to defend ourselves and the national economy, would simply fold overnight."

"And Russia, in a show of brotherhood steps in to help us out, by buying up all our infrastructure, our resources and our military technology. And, declaring war on terrorism, imposes martial law."

"Something like that, yes."

"That's pretty far-out. It can't be that easy."

"Do you know how many suitcases enter the United States every year?"

"I can't say—"

He didn't let me finish. "Approximately one hundred and sixty million. Perhaps substantially more."

I nodded. "Fine, but those which are lined with lead are easily detected, as are those that are radioactive."

"Don't be facetious, Alex. I tell you constantly. A good proportion of those cases do not enter by plane, but by boat or across our northern and southern borders in the trunks of cars or RVs. A device shipped to Mexico in a crate labeled 'Machine Parts' and then brought across the border in the back of an RV driven by a happy, perfectly normal, un-pierced, un-tattooed family devoid of large black beards and *capitis* dishcloths, would go completely undetected. As you well know."

"It's a needle in a haystack. Where do you start?"

"Precisely. That is the genius of the thing."

"I mean, we don't even know what we're looking for."

Nero held up two fat fingers. "We are looking for two things. One, a suitcase or a rucksack which is out of place and has been there too long."

"OK, but that's one for the cops and security firms."

"Two, signs that a bomb has been assembled or placed somewhere."

I nodded. "OK," I nodded some more, thinking, "and signs that loose ends have been or are being tidied up."

"Good, you are thinking of homicides."

"Because an operation like this is going to require too many people. If they just brought the real bomb in and deto-nated it that could be almost untraceable. But they don't want that. They want to subject society and the economy to a prolonged period of stress and fear, right?"

"Correct."

"So they are going to need, in addition to the team who bring in the suitcase with the real device, maybe ten or twelve more people to put together and place the dummies. That is a big operation. Each one of those people is a poten-tial loose end. My guess is they are going to be eliminating those loose ends just as soon as they have done their jobs. So that is somewhere to start. Unexplained murders, in any of our six locations, which occurred within the last week or ten days."

He pressed a button on his desk. Lovejoy's exquisite voice said, "Yes, sir?"

"I want a list of all unexplained murders in the last week in Maryland, Virginia and DC, New York City, the Silicon Valley area, Los Angeles, Texas and New Mexico. Alert the state police and the FBI, we are looking for murders of people who have hitherto been more or less anonymous, and whose murder is apparently without motive. Have you got that?"

"Yes sir."

We went silent for a moment. I tried to wrack my brain for any other sign we might look for. I said, "Obviously customs and shipping companies are on high alert, airlines, airport security..."

"Yes, all the standard stuff has been seen to." He hesitated a moment, then said, "Of course, my theory about DC may be completely wrong. The fact is that any of those targets will have a very similar effect. We cannot focus on any one of them. The plan is brilliant."

I nodded. "I know." I made to stand. "Sir, is there anything else I need to know?"

He shook his head. "No, I'll be in touch if anything turns up."

"I'm going to check with contacts and sources."

"Every little bit helps."

Out on the sidewalk I looked for a cab. The nocturnal city glowed amber, and drowned out the stars. For a moment I was assaulted by the nightmare vision of DC as a wrecked, blackened graveyard of twisted steel girders and crumbling concrete. It had happened to Nagasaki and to Hiroshima. People, normal families, couples, children, had been going about their daily lives. A plane had appeared far above them, in the sky; most of them hadn't even seen it. Its payload dropped from its belly while the children played and people chatted, and it never even reached the ground.

The transition from "normal everyday" to total annihilation had happened in fractions of a second.

Scan the QR code below to purchase RUSSIAN ROULETTE.
Or go to: righthouse.com/russian-roulette

NOTES

CHAPTER 7

1. See *Mason's Law*

CHAPTER 10

1. See *The Einstaat Brief* (Harry Bauer)

PROLOGUE

1. 1,945 miles